THE TV SHOW RIVAL

HER RIVAL SERIES
BOOK 3

EMILY HAYES

1

JAMIE

The insistent ring of her phone alarm made Jamie Nguyen wake up, and she swatted at it blindly to shut it up. With a groan that rivaled the rusty gate across the street, she rolled over and squinted at the pre-dawn light filtering through the blinds.

Ugh, 5:30 AM already.

She stretched sluggishly, the sleep clinging to her for a few precious moments before swinging her legs over the side of the bed. A gentle smile played on her lips as she heard a faint pop echoing from her lower back, making her wince at the familiar ache—a souvenir from yesterday's particularly vigorous vinyasa flow class. But the ache was a welcome reminder of her dedication to a healthy body and mind.

Today was going to be a good day, she could already feel it.

Reaching for her half-empty water bottle on the nightstand, she took a long, gulping drink. Hydration was key, as she always said to her clients.

As she stood up from the bed, her eyes caught her naked reflection in the full-length wall mirror.

Her shoulder-length dark hair was a cascade of glossy black waves, tied in a messy bun. Her features were delicate, with gray eyes, a small, straight nose and full lips that often curved into a smile.

Her years of healthy eating and an active life-style gave her the athletic body she was so proud of.

She put on her shorts and singlet and headed over to the small kitchen, where she began a ritual as familiar as her own breath.

The kettle hummed to life as she set about lighting a small bundle of sandalwood sticks that lay in a carved wooden holder. With practiced ease, she lit one, watching the flame dance before turning into a wisp of curling smoke that produced a sweet, smoky aroma.

This instantly transported her to her grandmother's tiny Hanoi apartment, where the scent had always mingled with the aroma of simmering pho.

She scooped a loose-leaf blend of chamomile and lavender from a cobalt blue tin into her favorite ceramic mug, adorned with swirling blue and white patterns. It was a present from her father last year on her 38th birthday.

Then she poured the steaming water over the herbs inhaling the fresh, calming scent as the delicate flowers unfurled in the hot liquid.

"Just what the doctor ordered," she whispered as she took sips.

Draining the last drops of chamomile tea, Jamie set the mug down with a satisfied sigh.

Today was packed. Not only did she have her usual morning class at the gym, but tonight she was leading a special workshop at a local community center, a chance to introduce the transformative power of yoga to a new group of people.

Images played behind her closed eyelids—the tentative smiles of new students, the hesitant creaks of unfamiliar bodies finding new positions, the eventual sighs of relief and accomplishment—they made her smile.

Unrolling her yoga mat in the center of the living room, she glanced at the small Zen garden she'd meticulously built on her windowsill—a miniature landscape of raked sand, smooth river stones, and a single bonsai tree.

"Alright, body. Time to find our center. Today's gonna be a doozy."

Taking a seat in lotus pose, Jamie brought her hands to her lap, palms facing up. With each inhale, she visualized a golden light filtering into her being, radiating outwards to encompass her entire being. Exhaling, she released any bad energy, letting it dissipate like the morning mist.

Moments melted into one another until a soft chime from her phone timer signaled the end of her meditation and she opened her eyes, feeling centered and grounded.

The morning sun glinted off the chrome of Jamie's Mazda as she pulled into the familiar parking lot of Zenith Fitness. Unloading her gym bag, the rhythmic thrumming of bass music from inside vibrated through the pavement.

Pushing open the doors, she was greeted by the therapeutic sounds of clanking weights and grunts of exertion. Her regulars, a motley crew of office workers, stay-at-home moms, and aspiring athletes, caught sight of her and waved enthusiastically.

Unlike the high-octane, boot-camp style some trainers favored, Jamie's sessions focused on mindful movement and long-term health.

"Alright everyone, gather around!" she called out, her voice warm and inviting.

Most people stopped their stretches and migrated towards the center of the room, where she stood next to a large whiteboard adorned with a colorful anatomical diagram.

"Today's session focuses on core strength and stability," she explained, grabbing a marker and circling a section of the illustration depicting the abdominal muscles.

"As we get older, our muscles can weaken, leading to back pain and decreased stability. These exercises will help strengthen those muscles from the inside out, improving your posture and overall well-being."

The session unfolded with a mix of body-weight exercises—planks, bridges, and modified side-lying leg raises. These were combined with yoga poses that focussed on core strength. Jamie wasn't a drill sergeant barking commands, but a patient mentor, ensuring their workout was effective, safe, and most importantly, enjoyable.

Spotting a group of friends struggling with medicine ball slams, she approached them.

"Hey guys, remember, core engaged! Use the power of your whole body, not just your arms."

There was nothing as satisfying as watching her clients push their limits, their faces flushed with exertion and smiles. This, she thought, was what it was all about—empowering people to take control of their well-being, not just through physical training, but through a holistic approach to mind and body.

"Great work, Sarah! Feel that burning sensation? That's your body getting stronger."

"Mark, remember to keep your back straight; slow and steady wins the race."

The atmosphere in the gym wasn't one of fierce competition but of camaraderie and mutual support. Clients offered each other high fives after completing challenging sets and groans of exertion were followed by shared laughter.

She walked towards a young woman, who was nervously fiddling with the weight settings on a leg press machine.

"Hey, Lynn, don't worry about setting that too high. Let's start with controlled reps and focus on form first, okay?"

Lynn, a petite brunette with glasses perpetually perched on the bridge of her nose, looked up with a shy smile. "Thanks, Jamie. I just, uh, don't want to make a fool of myself."

"The only way you make a fool of yourself is by giving up before you even try. Remember, strength isn't just about how much weight you lift. It's about pushing yourself, finding your limits, and then exceeding them."

With a patient hand, Jamie adjusted Lynn's posture on the leg press, guiding her through the first few reps. As her initial apprehension melted away, replaced by a focused determination, Jamie couldn't help but beam.

By the end of the class, a collective sense of accomplishment filled the room. Beads of sweat glistened on foreheads but smiles were even brighter.

As they packed up their belongings, Lynn approached her with a grateful smile. "I can finally hike without my knee acting up! Thank you, Jamie, you're a lifesaver."

Moments like these—witnessing the positive impact of her work—were what fueled her passion.

Jamie had chosen the Elmwood Center for a reason. Tucked away in a corner of the city with limited access to high-end gyms, it offered a welcoming space for those seeking a path towards well-being, regardless of their socioeconomic background.

Stepping into the designated workshop room, she surveyed the scene.

The walls were adorned with colorful murals depicting scenes of local landmarks and bulletin boards overflowed with flyers for everything from cooking classes to computer literacy workshops. It radiated a welcoming inclusivity that resonated deeply with Jamie's philosophy.

Folding chairs lined the hardwood floor, facing

a makeshift stage adorned with a beautiful portrait depicting a serene mountain landscape.

Dressed in comfortable yoga pants and a loose tank top, she walked up to the chalkboard at the front, grabbed a piece of chalk and wrote a simple inscription: "Find Your Inner Peace."

Smiling to herself, she added a small lotus flower beside the words. It was a symbol of growth, resilience, and the potential for beauty that bloomed within each of them.

A mix of ages and backgrounds filled the room, with curiosity on their faces.

Taking a deep breath, she began. "Hi everyone, and welcome to our Introduction to Mindfulness and Yoga workshop! My name's Jamie, and I'm so grateful you've all chosen to spend your evening here with me."

A smattering of applause filled the room, followed by a few shy smiles. She decided to start by dispelling the misconception that meditation and yoga were reserved for yogis contorted into pretzel shapes, making them laugh.

"You know, I wasn't always this calm and collected person you see in front of you. There was a time when anxiety was a constant companion, and my self-esteem was about as low as a deflated basketball."

She paused, allowing her words to sink in.

"But then I discovered yoga and meditation, at a tender age. It wasn't about forcing myself into impossible poses or clearing my mind completely. It was about learning to listen to my body, to quiet the chatter in my head, and to find a sense of peace within the chaos."

18 years ago...

Twelve-year-old Jamie chewed on her bottom lip, as she sat in class.

Today was the day of the big presentation—a project that she'd poured weeks of work into. But the thought of standing in front of the class, their expectant eyes burning into her face, made her stomach churn like a washing machine on high spin.

Images of her voice cracking, her mind going blank, the entire class erupting in laughter, flashed before her eyes. Her gaze darted around the room, seeking an escape route or a hidden corner where she could melt into invisibility before Ms. Cole, the new teacher, called.

"Jamie Nguyen, are you ready to wow us with your presentation?"

A loud snort cut through the air. "Great, is Scaredy-Cat Jamie really going to wow us today?" Marty sneered but cowered at Ms. Cole's stern look.

Shame burned through Jamie. She wasn't just "Scaredy-Cat" to Marty, the class bully; the nickname had become a chorus whispered behind her back since kindergarten.

"Jamie, take a deep breath. You've worked hard on this project."

Standing up felt like climbing Mount Everest. Her legs, shaky and uncoordinated, seemed determined to betray her. Reaching the front of the class, the room dissolved into a blur. All she could hear was the deafening roar of her own heartbeat.

"H-hello," she stammered. The carefully practiced words lodged themselves in her throat, refusing to come out. Then, her body began to tremble.

"Looks like someone's gonna throw up pretty soon," Marty snickered, eliciting laughter from his classmates.

"Marty! That's not how you treat your class-mates. Shame on you," Ms. Cole scolded.

A choked sob escaped Jamie's lips. Tears welled up in her eyes, blurring the already indistinct faces before her.

The teacher rushed to her side. "It's alright. Why don't you take a seat? We can try again another day."

As Jamie sank back into her chair, defeated and humiliated, tears continued to trace a path down her cheek.

The final school bell rang through the halls, and the students ran off with their schoolbags.

With her head hung low, Jamie shuffled towards the exit, still feeling embarrassed from the failed presentation and Marty's taunts.

Just as she walked through the hallway, a gentle hand touched her arm. Looking up, she met Ms. Cole's concerned gaze. Unlike the other adults who dismissed her anxieties as shyness, she saw the raw fear that engulfed the poor girl.

"Jamie, are you alright?"

She managed a watery nod.

"I wanted to talk to you about your presentation."

She flinched, bracing herself for a round of criticism. But Ms. Cole surprised her.

"You know, you have a brilliant mind. Your project on the water cycle was truly impressive."

Surprise sparked in Jamie's tear-filled eyes. No one had ever called her brilliant before. Except her parents probably.

"But it seems like you get very nervous when you have to present in front of the class."

Jamie nodded mutely, unable to voice the fear that choked her every time she faced a crowd.

Just then a familiar figure emerged, a woman with a striking resemblance to Jamie. It was Mrs. Nguyen.

"There you are, Jamie. What took you so long?"

"Hello, Mrs. Nguyen. I'm Kathy Cole, the new head teacher." She extends a handshake.

"Nice to meet you, Ms. Cole." Mrs. Nguyen shakes her hand.

"I wanted to talk to you about Jamie's performance in class. She is a truly bright girl, but she seems to struggle, especially in classroom settings."

Mrs. Nguyen's expression softened. "It's not just

presentations, Ms. Cole. Jamie has battled anxiety ever since she was little. She's very reserved and gets nervous in social situations."

"I'm sorry to hear that."

"The doctor diagnosed her with an anxiety disorder. She's been taking medication, but it doesn't always seem to help."

"Perhaps there are other avenues to explore. Have you ever considered something like yoga or meditation?"

"Yoga?"

"Yes," Ms. Cole confirmed, reaching into her pocket. "I know a wonderful yoga instructor who specializes in helping people, especially young ones, manage stress. Here's her card."

She handed the card to Mrs. Nguyen. "It might be worth a try."

"Thank you." Mrs. Nguyen glanced at Jamie. A seed of hope had been planted. Maybe, this yoga thing could be the key to unlocking a future where Jamie wouldn't be a prisoner of her own anxieties. She thought.

∾

Present Day...

"That day was a turning point, thanks to Ms. Cole's suggestion. And ever since, yoga has been a constant companion on my journey. I became a certified yoga instructor, driven by the desire to share this gift with others who were once like me."

Her gaze swept over the room, connecting with each participant. "Many of you here tonight might be struggling with similar challenges—feeling overwhelmed, stressed, or simply out of touch with yourselves. But I want you to know this: you are not alone. And through the practice of mindfulness and yoga, you can learn to manage stress and cultivate inner peace."

The room erupted in warm applause, and she smiled, genuinely touched by the response.

"So, let's begin. We'll start with some simple breathing exercises, focusing on grounding ourselves in the present moment. Close your eyes, take a deep breath through your nose, filling your belly with air. Hold it for a count of three, and then slowly exhale, releasing any tension you might be carrying."

The session ended and the workshop participants began to filter out. Jamie, stationed near the makeshift stage, greeted each person with a warm smile and a sincere, "Thank you for coming."

A couple caught her eye. Two men, probably in their late thirties, walked towards her, their hands clasped together. The taller man, with a neatly trimmed beard and warm brown eyes, spoke first.

"Hi, I'm Danny and this is my husband, Charles. I must say, that was incredible. We haven't felt this relaxed in ages."

Jamie smiled. This were exactly the kind of feedback she lived for. "I'm so glad to hear it, gentlemen."

Danny chuckled good-naturedly. "We might just have to become regulars at your workshops."

"That would be lovely. Do you mind sharing what's been stressing you?"

"Actually, it's wedding season. We officiate a lot of ceremonies this time of year, and the joy can be a bit... overwhelming sometimes," Charles, the shorter man with a kind smile and a touch of gray at his temples, said.

Jamie nodded in understanding. "Weddings are supposed to be happy occasions but planning them can definitely take a toll."

Danny agreed, pulling a business card from his pocket. "By the way, we own a small coffee shop downtown—The Daily Grind. If you're ever in the neighborhood, come on by for a free coffee. Consider it a thank you for the amazing workshop."

She accepted the card. "Thank you, that's very kind of you."

"You mentioned you're a certified yoga instructor, right?" Charles asked.

"Yes, I am. I offer private classes and group sessions at a few studios in the city."

"Maybe that's something we should look into, honey. A little couples' yoga retreat?" He nudged Danny.

"Well," she offered, handing them a business card with a warm smile. "If you're ever interested, you know where to find me."

"Thank you again, Jamie. You've truly inspired us," Danny said, accepting the card.

"We'll definitely be in touch," Charles added.

2

JESS

"Rise and shine, sleepyhead!" Mango, Jess Thompson's resident scarlet macaw, flew out of his stand in the living room into the bedroom, squawking and ruffling his crimson feathers.

The mischievous little terror had become her personal wake-up call ever since she'd adopted him a few years ago. No need for regular alarms because Mango right here, with his flamboyant squawks and insatiable curiosity, was the perfect way to start a day dedicated to helping others achieve their fitness goals.

With another loud squawk and a series of enthusiastic chirps, Mango perched on the edge of her nightstand.

Jess cracked open one eye, a groan escaping her lips. "Alright, alright, Mango. I hear you. Sunshine and rainbows comin' right up."

Mango tilted his head, regarding her with an intelligent glint in his beady black eyes. He squawked again, this time a series of clicks and whistles that Jess, through years of cohabitation, had come to interpret as a demand for a head scratch.

Smiling sleepily, she reached out a hand, offering him a gentle scratch behind his feathery crest. "You're such a tyrant, you know that?"

Despite the grumbling, she secretly cherished Mango's morning wake-up calls. They were a quirky reminder of the joyful chaos that came with being a pet owner.

With a sigh, she threw back the covers, and headed to the closet. There she shed off her pajamas for a well-worn tank top and a pair of capri leggings that hugged her curves in all the right places.

Getting to the kitchen, she glugged down a tall glass of cool water from the water dispenser, leaving her feeling rehydrated. Next, breakfast. Fueling her body was key, especially with a busy day of training ahead.

She whipped up a quick scramble of eggs and paired it with creamy avocado slices, and a slice of whole-grain toast completed the picture of a healthy and satisfying meal.

As she devoured her breakfast at the dining table, she glanced at Mango, who was now mimicking the sound of a kettle whistling, his head bobbing with each chirp. She laughed. Maybe a parrot alarm wasn't the most conventional choice, but it certainly added a touch of personality to her mornings.

Hitting the play button on her high-energy playlist, and pulling out a kettlebell, Jess transformed her living room into her own personal gym. A quick dynamic warmup got her blood flowing, followed by a series of exercises that challenged her strength and endurance.

Squats that burned in her quads, lunges that tested her balance, pushups that sent her arms screaming in protest; each repetition fueled by a quiet determination to stay ahead of the curve.

After an intense but exhilarating forty-five minutes, Jess collapsed onto her couch, chest heaving and breath ragged.

A quick trip to the shower and she was feeling refreshed and invigorated. Skincare came next, a simple routine of cleanser, moisturizer, and a touch of sunscreen.

Standing before her closet, Jess surveyed her options. She needed something comfortable enough to move in but also stylish enough to project an image of confidence and expertise.

She opted for a pair of sleek black yoga pants and a bright coral tank top, the color of a summer sunrise, added a pop of color. Finally, she tossed on a light zip-up jacket, perfect for layering throughout the day.

She slicked her hair back into a neat ponytail and applied light make up.

Comfortable? Check. Stylish? Absolutely. Most importantly, did she feel confident? A wide grin split her face. You bet she did.

She snapped some pics of herself for her instagram. Being a fitness influencer didn't come without constantly looking amazing and consistently putting herself out there.

With a final spritz of her favorite perfume, Jess grabbed her phone, and scrolled through her Instagram feed, pausing to admire a post featuring a client who had achieved incredible results. A quick comment of encouragement and a virtual high five later, Jess moved on to respond to direct messages.

Questions about workout routines, requests for meal plan advice, and heartfelt messages of gratitude—Jess took the time to answer each one, her fingers flying across the screen.

With a satisfied sigh, Jess locked her phone and headed towards the door. But on her way out, her gaze fell on a picture frame nestled on the wall. Inside, a younger Jess, beaming in a cap and gown, with a diploma clutched proudly in her hand.

On the certificate was written *Kinesiology and Sports Science*. This was a testament that the countless hours of studying and grueling exercises unlocked the door to a career she loved.

For a moment, she paused, the memory of that determined young woman coming to her mind...

12 years ago...

The rising morning sun beat across the patchy grass of a backyard in rural Ohio.

Fifteen-year-old Jess grunted with effort; her face contorted in a determined frown as she hoisted a weathered car tire off the ground. It wasn't a fancy gym weight, but it was the best she could scrounge from the local junkyard.

The backyard itself was a testament to their modest circumstances. A weather-beaten clothesline strung between two rickety wooden posts strained under the weight of mismatched laundry. A lopsided swing set, its once-vibrant red paint faded to a dull rust, stood abandoned in a corner.

The back door creaked open, and Jess' mom, Mrs. Sue Thompson, stepped into the yard. She was a woman worn thin by years of nightshifts at the local factory. She stopped short, her eyes widening at the sight of Jess straining against the tire.

"Jess, honey! What on earth are you doing?"

Jess lowered the tire with a huff, wiping a bead of sweat from her brow. "Hey, Mom! You're early." She tried for a casual tone, but the tremor in her voice betrayed her exhaustion.

She hurried towards her daughter, her gaze sweeping over Jess' reddened face and damp clothes. "It's almost seven, honey. You shouldn't be working yourself this hard."

"But Mom, I have to win the upcoming decathlon at school. The scholarship prize is the only way I can afford college for sports science."

Different emotions spread over her mom's face —pride, worry, and a deep ache of regret. She wasn't able to give Jess the opportunities she craved, the fancy equipment or the sleek gym memberships. All she had was the scrapyard tire and her unwavering love.

"Honey, I know how much this means to you. But you're pushing yourself too hard. What if you get hurt?"

Jess met her mother's gaze with a fierceness that mirrored Sue's own quiet strength. "I won't, Mom. I have to try hard. This is my chance, my only chance."

She reached out, her calloused hand gently cupping Jess' cheek. "I know, sweetie. And I'm so proud of you for chasing your dreams. Believe me, I am. I just wish I could do more to help." Her voice cracked slightly.

Jess squeezed her mother's hand. "You do more than you know, Mom. You work so hard to give me everything you can. It's enough. I promise."

A watery smile touched her lips. Wiping away a stray tear, she said, "Alright then, little athlete. Let's get you inside and make some breakfast."

Present Day...

Jess stood there for a moment, a nostalgic smile gracing her lips as she gazed at the picture on the wall. Those grueling dawn workouts, fueled by the desperate hope of a scholarship, had paid off in ways she could never have imagined, making her not just a fitness trainer but a sought-after fitness influencer.

With a renewed sense of purpose tucked away in her heart, she grabbed her car keys, ready to head out.

Mango, ever the observer, cocked his head, his black eyes gleaming with what could have been amusement. "Looking fierce, huh, little guy?"

She chuckled, ruffling his feathers playfully. "See you later, buddy. Let's go show those clients what real fitness is all about."

The crisp autumn air whipped through Jess' hair as she pulled into the parking lot of the outdoor fitness station. Her signature morning class, the aptly named "Morning Gruel," was notorious for separating the wheat from the chaff.

It was a high-intensity interval training session

designed to burn calories and leave participants begging for mercy (in the best way possible, of course).

Today's crew stood huddled in various states of anticipation—some with water bottles clutched tightly, others bouncing on the balls of their feet, ready for action.

Jess walked towards them, her smile radiating a confidence that bordered on intensity. Scanning the faces before her, she saw a mix of regulars— battle-hardened veterans sporting determined expressions—and some newbies.

"Alright, Gruelers! Ready to earn your break-fast? Don't come in here expecting a leisurely stroll. This is high-octane fitness, designed to drill you!"

A feel of nervous energy ran through the group, but Jess didn't flinch. Soft wasn't on the menu. Her clients weren't here for pats on the back; they were here for results, and she was the drill sergeant ready to deliver.

"...Let's loosen those rusty joints. High knees, people, higher! Feel the blood pumping, feel your body waking up!"

Each command was a rallying cry, coated with a tough love that brooked no excuses. Jumping jacks turned into burpees, high knees transitioned into lunges, each repetition executed with a focus on form and explosiveness.

"Harder! Show your body who's boss. Pain is temporary, quitting is forever!"

No time for self-pity, no room for excuses. She demanded effort, sweat, and the unwavering belief that they could conquer anything she threw their way.

By the end of the session, the group was a collective mess of sweat and exhilaration. Collapsed on the cool grass, some panted for breath, others wore triumphant grins that spoke volumes.

"Alright, warriors! You did good today. Remember, every drop of sweat, every burning muscle, is a step closer to the version of yourself you crave to be. Now, get some protein in those bellies, and come back for more tomorrow!"

3

_____

JAMIE

"Welcome, everyone, to today's cooking class, "Nourishing Your Mind and Body!" Today, we're going to whip up some delicious and healthy dishes that are not only good for your taste buds but also do wonders for your brainpower and mood." Jamie, a whirlwind of energy in a cheerful red apron, greeted her eager students with a warm smile.

A young woman raised her hand. "I'm always so sluggish in the afternoon. What can I eat to beat the slump?"

"Great question. Our bodies have a natural internal clock called the circadian rhythm. Eating breakfast jump starts your metabolism, like firing up the engine for the day. Think herbal tea, eggs or yogurt with berries—protein and healthy fats to keep you energized."

A gruff voice boomed from the back. "What about us folks who hate mornings? Coffee's my only friend before noon."

She chuckled. "Coffee can be a pick-me-up, but too much can lead to jitters and crashes later. You can supplement with a smoothie packed with power. Spinach, banana, almond milk, and a sprinkle of walnuts—a delicious way to get a dose of vitamins, healthy fats, and protein, all in one shot!"

His eyes widened. "A smoothie that doesn't taste like punishment? Sign me up!"

Everyone laughs.

"So, what foods should we avoid if we want to stay happy and focused?" someone asked.

"Excellent question. Our brains love healthy fats, found in fish like salmon or avocados. But processed foods and excessive sugar can trigger inflammation and even be linked to anxiety and depression. Think of it as feeding your brain the right kind of fuel for optimal performance."

As the class progressed, the kitchen buzzed with activity. Students chopped, whisked, and simmered, their conversation peppered with questions and excited discoveries.

One student, a busy professional with a packed schedule, confessed, "I always resort to grabbing fast food when I'm on the go. But it leaves me feeling sluggish afterwards."

"Sounds familiar, Emily. But with a little planning, you can make healthy choices on the go. Think pre-portioned snacks like veggie sticks with hummus or a handful of almonds. Easy, convenient, and good for your mood and energy levels."

"Water is our internal Uber, folks! It delivers nutrients to our cells and keeps everything running smoothly. Dehydration can zap our energy and focus, so let's keep those glasses filled!" she added.

Finally, the moment of truth arrived. The students gathered around the table, their faces gleaming with anticipation as Jamie revealed the spread: a vibrant lentil and quinoa salad with a creamy avocado dressing, a refreshing green smoothie bursting with spinach and berries, and a side of grilled salmon with roasted vegetables.

The savory scent hit Jamie like a warm hug as she finally unlocked the front door.

"Later than a Kardashian arriving fashionably late," a familiar voice boomed from the dining table.

Jamie rolled her eyes with a smile. Of course, it was her older brother, Mikey. At 41, he still had that mop of unruly brown hair that seemed permanently windblown, and his laughter lines crinkled around eyes that always held a hint of mischief. He was the family comedian, the life of the party, even if that party was just a Tuesday night dinner at their parents' place.

"Hey everyone!" Jamie called out, taking a deep breath of the fragrant air. The house was a sensory overload in the best way possible with the excited chatter of her siblings and that unmistakable aroma of home—lemongrass, fish sauce, and the promise of a delicious meal.

Beside Mikey sat her sister, Layla. At 36, she was the epitome of put-together. Her brown hair was styled in a sleek bob, with some jewelry high-lighting her beautiful skin. She was the organized one, the planner, the one who always remembered birthdays and anniversaries.

Across her, sat Alex, Jamie's youngest sibling.

His short, dark hair was dyed a vibrant shade of purple, a silent rebellion against the expectations of their sometimes-traditional Vietnamese family. He was 26 and an artist.

Jamie grinned, walking up to her dad at the head of the table. "Hi Dad. Sorry I'm late, traffic."

Mr. Nguyen smiled, happy to see her. His weathered hands, strong from years of hard work, reached out to embrace her. He had salt and pepper hair, thanks to being in his middle sixties.

Her mom, Mai, a petite woman bustled out of the kitchen, a steaming pot of canh chua ca (fish sour soup) balanced precariously in her hands. In her early sixties, she still looked young and bubbly even though a few silver lines showed on her hair.

"Hi Mom." She kissed her.

"Don't mind your brother, Jamie. He just likes to pretend he's not the one who always keeps us waiting." Her Vietnamese accent was softer now, years of living in America smoothing out the edges, but the warmth in her voice remained constant.

"Oh come on!" Mikey raises his hand in exasperation.

"Mikey, have you forgotten who Mom's favorite

kid is? Don't mess with the golden child, you hear?" Layla, the instigator, says with sarcasm.

Of course, she was always in cahoots with Mikey. Their bond, forged through countless childhood pranks on Jamie and Alex, was as strong as ever.

But Alex cleared his throat. "Hold on a second, Layla. If Jamie's Mom's golden child, have you forgotten how clingy you are to Dad?" He knew exactly how to push Layla's buttons.

"Oh please. I'm not a clingy child anymore, Alex. I'm all grown up." She rolled her eyes.

"Yet you almost cried when Dad didn't say 'I love you' on your birthday." He winked at Jamie, knowing fully well they were both buying into the rivalry Sarah and Mikey had going.

That's Alex and Layla for you, Jamie thought with a smile. Always bickering and bantering, but a united front when it truly mattered.

Mom chuckled. "Enough teasing, you lot! There's plenty of love to go around in this family. Let's enjoy our dinner before it gets cold."

As chopsticks danced over steaming bowls of food, a hush fell over the table. Layla cleared her throat making all eyes turn to her.

"So, there's something I wanted to share..." She

paused as though to build suspense before continuing, "I'm engaged!"

The room erupted in cheers and congratulations. Mom, already wiping happy tears from her eyes, reached across the table and squeezed Layla's hand. "Oh, honey, that's wonderful news! We're so happy for you!"

"Thanks, Mom!"

"We have so much to plan! The venue, the dress..." Mom trailed off.

"Congratulations, kiddo! We're so happy for you." Dad smiles.

Jamie, her heart overflowing with joy for her sister, reached across the table and squeezed her hand. "I'm so thrilled for you, Layla! Tell us everything!"

The evening transformed into a celebration of her upcoming nuptials. Stories flowed, memories were shared, and laughter filled the space.

Amidst the chatter, Mom turned towards Jamie. "Now, Jamie, with a wedding to plan, we need to make sure everyone looks their best." Her gaze landed on Mikey, who was polishing off his second bowl of rice. "Maybe you can help your brother shed a few pounds before the big day?"

Mikey groaned theatrically. "Here we go again

with the health lectures. Can't a guy enjoy a slice or two in peace?"

"You should really consider joining Jamie's healthy eating bandwagon so you wouldn't be looking a little...rounder on Layla's big day, would you?"

"Mom, I'm chubby, maybe, but don't talk like I'm obese? Come on!"

"Oh please. Have you seen your belly lately? I almost mistook you for your pregnant cousin Linh!"

The room erupted in laughter, Mikey included.

Dad, ever the peacekeeper, chuckled. "Mai, leave the boy alone. I'm sure girls love a guy with a little extra padding."

Mom snorted. "You wish! Ask Jamie here, she knows what girls really like—abs and muscles!"

"But it didn't rank first for you, did it, Mai? You used to say you liked my 'teddy bear' build."

He winked at Mom, who swatted his arm. "Don't twist my words, old man! I was just trying to boost your confidence."

"Are you saying you lied about liking my belly?"

Mom rolled her eyes. "That's besides the point!"

"Mom, isn't that hypocritical? You hate my brother's belly but love Dad's?" Layla says.

Jamie, seeing an opportunity to support both Mom and Mikey's health, jumped in. "I mean, maybe all those late-night pizzas and the beer aren't doing you any favors, bro."

Mikey, predictably, wasn't thrilled. "Can't all be wasting our days with woo woo yoga and kale smoothies like you little sis! I like to live a little."

The bickering and teasing continued throughout the rest of the meal.

Jamie knew they all loved each other and nobody really cared about Mikey's belly.

4

JESS

With a forkful of fluffy scrambled eggs demolished, Jess attacked the mountain of crispy bacon with a satisfied grunt.

It was a well-deserved post-torture breakfast, especially after witnessing the glorious display of agony (and eventual triumph) on the training field.

With her phone propped against a water bottle, she grabbed a napkin and dabbed at the corner of her mouth, scrolling through the morning feed.

Speaking of which... I should make a post.

Checking through her phone's gallery, a wicked grin split her face. There it was—the money shot.

Five trainees, faces contorted in a mixture of pain and determination, heaving a massive tractor tire across the finish line. Mud splattered, clothes clinging like second skins, but pure elation shining through sweat-streaked eyes.

This video needed a caption that captured the raw intensity of the session, a caption that sparked a fire in the hearts of those seeking true fitness. Or maybe ruffle some feathers in the "gentle cardio" crowd, because they gotta learn.

With a rogue grin on her face, her fingers danced across the screen.

"This is what peak performance looks like. There's a reason they call it boot camp, not nap camp. This, my friends, is what real results look like. Boot camp: where excuses are left in the mud. Sorry, not sorry to all the downward-dog lovers out there. #bootcamplife #earnyourbreakfast #realfitness"

Hitting post, she braced herself for the inevitable online firestorm.

Some might scoff at the lack of kale smoothies and sunrise jogs in her training methods, but hey, results spoke louder than trendy diets.

Her trainees weren't there for leisurely strolls in the park; they were there to get pushed, and that grueling tire flip was just one testament to their grit. Besides, the pure, unadulterated joy on their faces after they crossed that finish line? That was the real reward.

Yeah, they might curse her name under their breath now, fueled by the lingering burn of lactic acid, (especially for the newbies) but deep down, they knew they were getting stronger, fitter, and more badass by the day. And that, to her, was a beautiful thing.

She leaned back, savoring the warmth of the bacon and the knowledge that somewhere out there, someone was scrolling through their feed, seeing this picture, and feeling that spark of determination ignite.

Maybe they'd ditch the smoothie and join her in the mud tomorrow. Or maybe they'd scoff and stick to their comfort zone.

Either way, the message was out there. Boot camp wasn't for everyone, but for those who dared to embrace the challenge, the rewards were undeniable.

The notification bell on her phone pinged like a victory gong or should she say a startling pistol.

Clearly, her little caption must have struck a nerve. Comments rolled in faster than she could devour bacon.

"Haha. Well, time to see the fallout from my little controversy," she said to herself.

She scrolled through the comments to see a few fire emojis and cheers from her regulars. A couple of raised eyebrow emojis—those must be the yoga bunnies she secretly loved to rile up a bit. Healthy debate was good, kept things interesting.

The first comment popped up.

"Preach!"

"See? Some people get it." She smirked.

Next, a comment with a string of fire emojis: *"YOU SAID IT! Boot camp is where it's at! Downward-doggers need not apply!"*

She could practically hear the bicep-flexing emoji guy through the screen.

She added a high-five emoji for good measure. "Gotta support my boot camp brethren."

The debate raged on. More strings of fire emojis and support from her boot camp regulars filled the comment section.

A guy with a profile pic of him doing a handstand replied, *"Respect the bootcamp grind, but gotta* say, my core's pretty strong from all those inversions too."

"Touché, handstand dude, touché." Maybe she could give yoga a whirl sometime... Or never. She giggled at own joke.

One comment, dripping with sarcasm, read: *"Because true strength is only measured in sweat puddles and tractor tires, right?"*

She snorted. "Alright, internet stranger, hit me with your best shot."

Then, she tapped out a reply with a playful jab, *"Hey, don't knock the tractor tires till you try 'em! They build character... and biceps."*

Another comment popped up, this one from a seemingly neutral observer: *"Hmm, maybe there's room for both bootcamp and yoga in a well-rounded routine?"*

This one made her pause. Maybe they were onto something... nah. Probably not. She left them a winking emoji.

But then came the fun part.

SunshinenSmiles: *"Boot camp? More like boot camp for your ego, Jess! ♀ Yoga builds strength AND flexibility, try it sometime."*

She scoffed, picturing someone trying to hurl a tractor tire in Lululemon leggings.

"*Bless your heart, SunshinenSmiles, some of us need actual weights, not scented candles, to see results. #sorrynotsorry* ♀"

Some comments were downright nonsensical, like this one:

Muscle_Confusion: "*Wow, Jess, projecting much? Maybe you're just jealous you can't touch your toes.*"

She laughed so hard she almost choked. "He sounds as confused as his name and I'm already picturing a scrawny dude in his basement typing furiously."

"*Boot camp is SO 2010, Jess. Yoga builds strength AND flexibility. #balancedfitness*"

She rolled her eyes. "Balanced? More like boring-and-bland fitness."

Then she typed. "*Flexibility is great, until you gotta hurdle a fire pit, Karen. #priorities*"

"*Boot camp is intense, but isn't there a risk of injury? Maybe some low-impact stuff for recovery?*"

She paused. This comment required a more strategic response.

"*Absolutely! Rest and recovery are crucial. Boot camp can be modified for all fitness levels, and we always focus on proper form to minimize risk. #smarternotjuststronger,*" she typed in response.

The back-and-forth continued to blow up the

comment section, a hilarious mix of support, jabs, outrage, and the occasional misguided critique.

She scrolled through them all, thoroughly entertained. This was way more engaging than watching paint dry, which seemed to be the highlight of most fitness influencers' feeds.

As she finished cleaning her plate, the satisfaction she felt went beyond the delicious breakfast. It was the satisfaction of stirring the pot, of starting a conversation about fitness that went beyond the usual cardio bunny routines.

"Bring on the comments, people! Boot camp Jess is ready for anything you throw her way."

Friday night traffic proved a breeze compared to the usual weekday crawl. The beat-thumping music and celebratory playlist she had on full blast drowned out the honking and impatience.

Operation Surprise Mom was officially a go! Theo, bless his secretive heart, had managed to keep a poker face the entire week.

Even Riley, that ten-year-old walking spoiler alert, was surprisingly tight-lipped. Maybe all those spy movies they watched were finally paying off? Either way, she couldn't wait to see the look on Mom's face.

Her mom truly deserved the best. Raising her as a single mom at what, like, nineteen? Yeah, not easy. She remembered the late nights working double shifts, the ramen nights, the hand-me-downs from distant relatives, and the sheer exhaustion planted on her mom's face some days.

But her mom never let it dim her light. She'd still manage a smile and a warm hug even when the world felt like it was crumbling around them. Now, she was finally in a position to show her some appreciation, a fraction of what her mom had given her, and her heart swelled with pride knowing she could finally do something special for her.

Speaking of special, Theo was a keeper. When they met, he'd just lost his wife, and Riley was barely five.

Seeing her mom find love again, a love that's as strong and steady as an oak tree, filled Jess with a joy she couldn't describe.

Remembering how nervous her mom was to ask for her approval for their marriage made her chuckle. As if she wouldn't be over the moon for anything that made her mom happy! Let's just say the waterworks started flowing faster than Niagara Falls after she gave her mom a giant hug (and maybe a couple of tissues).

Her mom had been on a mini business trip to Portland to source unique handmade goods for her boutique and she was coming back today to a big surprise. Well, a small party.

Now, the waiting game. Anticipation simmered like a forgotten pot on the stove. She could practically hear the doorbell chime in her head, announcing her mom's arrival.

"Come on, traffic, clear up already! I can't wait to see the look on her face. That's the reward!"

The doorknob rattled, with the sound of jingling keys slicing through the tense silence.

Then, the door clicked open, and the door creaked a hesitant welcome.

"Light! Now!" she whispered, and Theo threw on the switch. Then, a collective yell of "Surprise!" exploded from behind the furniture.

Sue froze, framed in the doorway. The travel fatigue melted away, replaced with pure shock. Her eyes widened to cartoonish proportions, luggage sitting at her side.

Her features, once marked with the lines of worry and struggle during her time as a single mother, were smoother, healthier, revealing a woman perhaps a decade younger.

She looked beautiful in her flowery blouse and tight pants that skimmed her curves with a newfound elegance. Her once dull brown hair, sparkled with a healthy vibrancy, cascading down her shoulders in loose waves.

The surprise must have hit her all at once: the garish "Happy 48th Birthday!" banner strung across the living room, the explosion of rainbow streamers clinging desperately to the furniture, the gaggle of them—Jess, Theo, and Riley—sporting the most ridiculous birthday hats.

But the centerpiece, the undeniable star of the show, was the cake. A magnificent three-tiered monstrosity frosted in her favorite shade of chocolate, with a few candles on top.

It was a masterpiece, courtesy of Theo's secret mission to the bakery down the street (bless him for indulging Jess' slightly outrageous cake vision).

Before Sue could even sputter out a single

word, ten-year-old Riley decided this was the perfect moment for his own grand gesture.

He scurried forward with the solemnity of a knight bestowing a royal honor and draped a homemade garland of wildflowers around her neck while giggling uncontrollably. The lopsided construction, a chaotic blend of dandelions and clover, somehow managed to look adorable.

She blinked, the shock finally giving way to a smile that could light up the entire neighborhood.

She let out a shaky laugh, tears welling up in her eyes. "Oh my gosh, you guys! This is... incredible!"

They erupted in cheers, engulfing her in a giant hug, the flowery garland threatening to topple under the weight of their combined love.

"Happy birthday, Mom," Jess whispered, squeezing her tight.

"You guys... you really got me!" Her eyes, still sparkling with surprise, darted playfully around the room. "I knew it had to be your idea, Jess. You couldn't resist a good surprise party, could you?"

Jess grinned sheepishly. "Guilty as charged. But everyone was in on it, even Riley here."

Riley, still nestled in Mom's hug, piped up, "Nope! I didn't know anything!" His eyes widened innocently, completely betraying the mischievous glint that had been there earlier.

Riley looked just like his father. His dark curls bounced with each wiggle. He was constantly bursting with ideas and ready to jump into any adventure, often without considering the consequences.

Despite the occasional mess, Riley's infectious enthusiasm and genuine sweetness made him impossible to resist. His clothes, a mismatched assortment of comfy fabrics—a favorite Star Wars t-shirt tucked into pajama bottoms with mismatched socks—spoke volumes about his love for comfort and his tendency to prioritize fun over tidiness.

Mom threw her head back and laughed, wiping away another tear. "Oh, you little rascal! You kept calling me while I was away, asking where I was. I thought you just missed me!"

Riley squirmed free and puffed out his chest, striking a heroic pose. "Well, of course I missed you! But I also had an important job to do, Operation Surprise Mommy!"

They all laughed. As the laughter subsided, Sue turned to Theo, her gaze filled with admiration. "And you, Mr. Poker Face! I didn't suspect a thing."

Theo grinned, his crooked crown finally giving way and tumbling to the floor with a soft plop. "See, honey? I told you my acting skills were award-worthy!"

In his fifties, Theo sported a crown of black hair peppered with streaks of silver, particularly noticeable in his salt and pepper beard. He wasn't built like a fitness model, more stout than muscular, with a bit of a potbelly that jiggled good-naturedly when he laughed.

But what he lacked in sculpted abs, he more than made up for in warmth and kindness. Beneath his faded jeans and well-worn T-shirts, his calmness, a stark contrast to his wife's sometimes fiery personality, was one of the things his family loved most about him.

"And you managed to fool me."

Theo threw his hands up in mock defense. "Hey, I'm just a dedicated husband following orders." He winked at her, earning a playful nudge from her elbow.

The warm, familial energy in the room was palpable. This was exactly what Jess hoped for—a night filled with surprise, laughter, and love.

Sue deserved every bit of it and seeing herself surrounded by the people who cherished her most filled her heart with a joy that rivaled the sparkle of the candles on the cake.

"Alright, alright," Sue announced, wiping away a stray tear. "Enough with the waterworks! Let's get this party started. I can't wait to see what kind of trouble you've all gotten yourselves into with these decorations."

Jess winked. "Just wait, Mom. Tonight's all about you."

With that, it was time to tackle the magnificent cake. They ushered her towards it, singing a slightly off-key rendition of "Happy Birthday" to celebrate the incredible woman who brought them all together.

Taking a deep breath, Sue closed her eyes and made a silent wish. Then a single puff of air extinguished the candles, and the room erupted in applause.

Still beaming, she leaned over and gave Theo a lingering kiss. Riley and Jess, ever the enthusiastic scene-stealers, chimed in with a groan.

"Ugh, get a room, you two!" they teased in unison. Sue and Theo laughed, the blush creeping up Theo's neck, a dead giveaway.

The music started pumping, and soon the house was filled with dancing, laughter, and the joy of a family celebrating a very special birthday. As the evening unfolded, stories were shared, games were played, and the cake was devoured with gusto.

"Alright. Let's move on to the food. We've got a feast waiting over there. We figured you'd be famished after your trip," Jess said.

Mom's eyes widened. "A feast, you say? Don't tell me Theo and Riley whipped something up? I'm impressed they didn't burn down the kitchen."

"Hey, we know our way around the kitchen," Theo protested.

"When it comes to boiling water or toasting bread, sure."

Jess laughed. "Don't worry. It's mostly my handiwork. Although, Theo did help with the grilling, and Riley... he was in charge of taste-testing."

"Theo and Riley helping with the cooking? Now that's a sight I'd pay to see."

They laughed.

"Ready?" Jess asked.

Mom let out a hearty laugh. "Of course. Well,

as long as it's not another one of your *healthy experiments*, I'm game for anything."

"Relax," she assured, wrapping an arm around her shoulder. "It's nothing too... radical. Mostly your favorites. You know, the kind that doesn't involve tofu or kale chips. Tonight, we celebrate with all the deliciousness you deserve. No deprivation allowed."

Mom snorted. "Oh, that's a relief. Remember the time you tried to convince me tofu scramble was actually eggs?"

They both burst out laughing, the memory of her early attempts at vegan cooking still a source of amusement (and possibly slight horror) for her mom. Her face as she bravely took a bite of her "experimental" creations was a memory Jess held close.

There was that time she tried to make a vegan shepherd's pie with lentils that resembled a bowl of brown mush, or the healthy birthday cake that tasted suspiciously like cardboard. Thankfully, her culinary skills have improved significantly since then.

She gestured towards the dining table, laden with an impressive spread of food. "Behold! A feast fit for a queen, or at least a very special birthday girl."

"Wow, you guys went all out! This looks amazing."

5

JAMIE

Jamie had gone for stylish but sophisticated in her outfit—a black jumpsuit that loosely highlighted her body.

She finished the look with a spritz of her favorite perfume, the scent lingering in the air like a promise of an unforgettable night.

She was meeting Amy for a date, finally. It felt like forever since they last hung out. With Amy's recent MIA streak, dating her sometimes felt like dating a ghost; she knew Amy was out there somewhere, but good luck getting ahold of her.

Ugh, don't even get her started.

Like that time they planned a weekend getaway to that charming cabin in the woods. She spent weeks fantasizing about cozy nights by the fireplace, picking out the perfect outfit, prepping a basket full of gourmet snacks, and even booked a couples massage.

The day of the trip rolled around, and guess who was a no-show at the pick-up point? Yep, Amy. No call, no text, nada. Just her standing there like a lovesick fool with a picnic basket.

She texted Amy a dozen times, called even more, only to receive a text at 2 am the next day saying her "aunt's llama had an emergency and would reschedule soon." Seriously? Soon never came anyways.

Then came the whole birthday fiasco. Jamie spent ages planning a surprise party for her, complete with a scavenger hunt leading to her favorite bakery for a custom cake. She even wrangled her closest friends to keep it under wraps.

The big day arrived, and she practically vibrated with excitement all day, waiting for her reaction. Finally, the clock struck 8 PM, the designated party time. She texted the first clue, heart pounding in her chest... crickets.

Nothing. An hour later, still nothing. By the time her friends started dropping disappointed goodbyes, a cold dread had settled in her stomach. Turns out, Amy was at some random concert, completely forgetting about their plans (or so she claimed).

And then there was the "work conference" that kept Amy away for three straight days, her replies to Jamie's texts were a curt "busy" followed by radio silence. By day three, Jamie was pretty sure she was dating a secret agent with a penchant for disappearing acts.

But tonight, Amy swore she was all hers. No emergencies, no conferences, just them. Maybe this time would be different.

Pushing those anxieties aside, Jamie focused on the positive. Amy had a way of sweeping her off her feet when she was around. Her laugh was infectious, her smile could melt glaciers, and those eyes... Okay, Jamie, focus! She didn't want to appear desperate.

Chewing her lip, she ran the brush once more through her hair, she thought maybe tonight, Amy would actually show up, be present, and this rollercoaster of a relationship would finally find its tracks.

Taking a deep breath, she snagged her purse and headed out the door, hoping this date wasn't another rendezvous with Amy's invisibility cloak.

Pushing open the restaurant door, a wave of warm light and enticing aromas welcomed Jamie.

She scanned the room, searching for a head of familiar cropped cut auburn hair. And there she was. Amy sat tucked away in a corner booth, her brow furrowed in concentration as she studied the menu.

A surprised laugh escaped her lips. This was new. She glanced down at her watch: 7:50 PM. Amy was ten minutes early? Was this some kind of alternate universe? Usually, she was the one left fuming at the bar while Amy's "traffic nightmare" or "sudden work meeting" stretched on for hours.

Shaking off the remnants of past frustrations, she approached the table with a wide smile. However, she couldn't help but admire the way the soft lighting played over Amy's features, highlighting the sharp angles of her jawline and the flecks of gold that danced within her hazel eyes.

Amy was a striking woman, her wiry frame belying a strength Jamie could sense radiating from her. Her signature jade ring, a chunky cabochon carved with swirling green veins, gleamed on her middle finger, the only piece of jewelry interrupting the casual elegance of her outfit. Ripped jeans, the perfect shade of worn-in denim, hugged her toned legs, while an oversized white blouse hung loosely over a fitted black tank top, hinting at the powerful muscles sculpted beneath.

Amy's head snapped up, then, a genuine smile bloomed on her face.

"Jamie!" She rose for a hug, the familiar scent of her vanilla perfume filling her senses. A quick peck on the cheek, and she slid into the seat opposite her.

"Wow, you're actually early," Jamie blurted out before she could filter her thoughts. "That's a first."

"Well, I was already in the neighborhood, so I figured I'd drop in early," Amy explained casually.

"In the neighborhood, huh?" Her eyebrow quirked up.

The part of her that had been burned before couldn't help but dissect Amy's words. Wouldn't *missed you and wanted to see you* have been a more natural response?

It felt like maybe this date wasn't a pre-planned event on Amy's calendar, a night she'd been eagerly anticipating. Perhaps it was a spur-of-the-moment decision, and their meeting was a matter of convenience, not genuine desire.

The thought stung a little, a flicker of doubt threatening to cloud the joy of seeing Amy. But she pushed it down, forcing a smile. Tonight, she chose to believe in the possibility of a genuine date, a night where missed connections and last-minute cancellations were a thing of the past.

"Well, I'm glad you did. It's good to see you, Amy."

The waiter was a young man, impeccably dressed in a crisp, white shirt and black trousers. His posture was upright, and his dark hair was neatly styled. His brown eyes sparkled with a friendly warmth as he approached their table.

Amy confidently rattled off her order, a gourmet salad with a vinaigrette dressing. When it was Jamie's turn, she scanned the menu, then finally pointed to a dish that sounded appealing— a hearty pasta primavera with a creamy pesto sauce.

"You sure about that?" Amy wrinkled her nose, a hint of something unsettling crossing her features.

Jamie bristled a little. "Yeah, I'm sure. I love pesto."

"But the smell. It can be disgusting. Have you considered the seared scallops with lemon risotto? Much lighter, and the presentation is divine."

Before she could voice her protest, Amy leaned across the table, a saccharine smile plastered on her face.

"Why don't I just order that for you? I can't stand the smell of strong-flavored dishes."

The heat rose in her cheeks as she forced a smile. Part of her wanted to stick to her guns, to assert her own culinary preferences. But another, more unsettling part, recoiled at the thought of causing a scene or disappointing Amy.

The waiter raised an eyebrow in question, pen hovering over his notepad.

Amy placed Jamie's order to the waiter, adding her own suggestions for sides. He scribbled it down with a nod, leaving her feeling like a bewildered bystander in her own date night.

A cold realization hit her. In all this time, did she even know Amy? They'd been on "dates" for months, exchanged texts, sure, stolen a few kisses, but beyond that surface layer, there was a gaping hole.

She didn't know Amy's favorite movies, her childhood dreams, or even her preferred meal. And tonight, the biggest revelation of all—Amy's complete disregard for her choices, masked by a veneer of concern.

The arrogance in Amy's tone, the dismissive way she treated her initial selection, made the nervous flutter that used to be excitement now feel more like apprehension.

Maybe the universe was trying to tell her something with all those "llama emergencies." Maybe this date, like so many others that never materialized, was a sign that Amy wasn't the right fit for her after all.

For the first time, she saw Amy clearly. The charming girl who captivated her might have been a facade all along. Maybe the real Amy was the one sitting across from her now—controlling, judgmental, and utterly selfish.

The question wasn't whether tonight would be the start of something real. The real question was, did she even want it to be?

The meals arrived, sizzling and fragrant. For a moment, the awkward tension was forgotten as Jamie dug into the juicy goodness.

But across from her, Amy launched into a monologue about her recent trip to Barcelona that grated on her nerves.

She threw out names of trendy restaurants, boasted about exclusive clubs she managed to weasel her way into, and described the designer clothes she "had to have" while there. She described tapas crawls and flamenco shows, her voice brimming with self-importance.

With each passing minute, Jamie's frustration mounted. Amy hadn't even glanced her way the entire time, oblivious to her silence and the growing storm brewing behind her frown.

Didn't she see the way Jamie clenched and unclenched her jaw with each clink of her cutlery against the plate?

Apparently not. Amy's world revolved solely around her. Her experiences, her preferences, her opinions; all delivered in a monologue that could rival Shakespeare himself.

Finally, Jamie couldn't take it anymore. The fork clattered onto her plate, and the jarring sound momentarily halting Amy mid-sentence.

Amy blinked, startled. "Isn't the food good?"

The question provoked a surge of anger that nearly choked Jamie. "The food? The food is perfect. But some company that isn't a self-absorbed narcissist would be the real improvement," she said, her voice tight with barely suppressed emotion

The words wiped the smile finally off Amy's face. For a moment, there was only stunned silence, then a slow flush crept up her neck.

"What do you mean?" she sputtered, her wounded pride showing.

"You know exactly what I mean. This entire night has been about you, your trips, your preferences. Have you even asked me a single question about my life?"

For the first time that night, a genuine emotion crossed Amy's eyes. Was it anger, hurt, or the fear of losing control? It didn't matter.

Tonight wasn't about her anymore. Tonight was about Jamie realizing that self-absorption wasn't a charming quirk, it was a personality red flag she couldn't ignore.

"You haven't even noticed I haven't spoken a word in ten minutes, have you?"

"I just assumed you must be tired from work."

"No, Amy. I'm not tired. I'm simply... disappointed."

A frown creased Amy's brow. "Disappointed? Why?"

"Because in all this talk about you, your trips, your clothes... there hasn't been a single question about me, about my day, about anything other than yourself. This isn't a date; it's an audience with Queen Amy," Jamie retorted.

"Oh please. Why are you making such a fuss? If you wanted to talk about your day, you should have just said something!"

The audacity of her statement made Jamie's head reel. "Is this what you call a relationship, Amy? You showing up whenever you're *in the neighborhood* after vanishing for weeks on end on your self-indulgent trips, probably funded by your father's inheritance? You rarely respond to my messages, let alone pick up my calls!"

Amy's voice hardened to match her eyes. "Well, if that's what you want, fine! I can take you on those tours, call you, text you...Is that what will make you happy?"

Jamie stared at her, her heart sinking lower with each word. "Is that it, Amy? A performance? This isn't about making me happy, it's about a basic level of respect and communication. You know, the things that actual couples do?"

Taking a deep breath of exasperation, she asked, "Do you even love me, Amy?"

"Of course I do!" Amy replied defensively.

"Do you see a future with me? Getting married?"

A scoffing laugh escaped Amy. "Marriage? Please, Jamie. That's so cliché. I'm not getting tied down!"

The finality in her voice cut deep. Here it was, the truth laid bare. Jamie wanted to build a life, share dreams, maybe even have a white picket fence someday. Amy, on the other hand, seemed content traversing the globe, with no room for commitment in her life.

"Well, I want to get married someday, and apparently, that's not something you're interested in."

"Look," Amy sighed, trying to regain control of the situation, "Maybe in the future... We're still getting to know each other, right?"

"Getting to know each other? Amy, what's my favorite flower?"

A hesitant answer came back: "Lilies."

"Wrong. I'm allergic to flowers. If you ever

bothered to pay attention, maybe you would have known that.

She opened her mouth to retort, but Jamie held up a hand, silencing her.

"This isn't working. We're strangers cloaked in the illusion of a relationship. You haven't even bothered to learn the basics! I deserve better than this one-sided charade."

A desperate plea darted in Amy's eyes. "Wait, Jamie—"

But Jamie was done waiting. Done hoping that the girl who captivated her would magically reappear.

"Don't call me," Jamie cut her off, her voice leaving no room for argument. "Don't text me. And for heaven's sake, just stay away."

Jamie stood to leave but delivered one last parting shot. "And by the way, interrupting someone's order because a meal *smells* is not only inconsiderate, it's incredibly rude."

With that, Jamie walked out of the restaurant, leaving the self-absorbed narcissist behind.

The night may not have ended as she'd hoped, but it ended with a truth revealed. And that, she realized, was far better than clinging to a fantasy.

Pulling out her phone, Jamie shot Marty a quick text.

Hey, I'm coming over for the weekend. How about you, me, some peace and quiet (and hopefully some fish)? Pyramid Lake?

A grin spread across her face as the reply popped up almost instantly.

Sounds like a plan, J. Haven't missed a good catch in ages! And I look forward to hosting you here. See you at the lake.

As she climbed into her car, the engine came to life like a promise. This weekend was all about her, no more disappearing girlfriends or self-centered dates.

She punched in the GPS coordinates—destination: Pyramid Lake.

It had been months since she last cast a line there, a place that held a special kind of magic for her.

Back then, it was an escape, a place where the only company she craved was the gentle lapping of waves against the shore and the tug of a fighting fish on her line. And who was always by her side, net in hand and an evil spark in his eyes?

Marty, the class bully.

The very thought brought a smile to her lips. If you'd told her grade-school self that the class bully would become her closest confidante, she'd have scoffed at the notion.

Yet, here they were, two people who'd grown past the awkwardness of adolescence, forging a genuine friendship despite the past.

College brought them together again, an awkward apology on his part and a hesitant forgiveness from hers. But that was all it took. They discovered a shared passion for the outdoors, for the quiet thrill of the hunt (or in their case, the fish).

Pyramid Lake became their haven, a place where the troubles of the world faded away with each cast of the line. They spent countless lazy afternoons there, the gentle rocking of the boat a soothing counterpoint to the thrill of a tug on the fishing line.

Marty, surprisingly adept at the art of angling, had patiently taught her the art of casting, of reading the water, of respecting the delicate balance of the ecosystem. They'd return with stringers full of fish, enough for a celebratory campfire feast.

But his circumstances were different now. Married, with a little one on the way. No more impromptu fishing trips, she understood. But thankfully, he would be there this time.

The sun beat down, turning the surface of the lake into a shimmering expanse. The surrounding landscape was a mix of rocky terrain and sparse vegetation, with the occasional desert plant dotting the arid landscape. In the distance, the rugged mountains framed the scene, their peaks standing tall against the horizon.

Jamie sat on the weathered wooden dock that extended into the lake, its planks warmed by the sun. She wore a wide-brimmed hat to shield her face from the intense sun, a pair of comfortable pants, and sturdy boots, ready for any outdoor adventure.

The dock creaked slightly under her weight as she leaned back against the rail, taking in the peaceful surroundings.

Her bobber sat stubbornly still, mirroring her lack of success. Another cast, another plop, and another sigh escaped her lips. Maybe the fish here had all grown wise to her rusty techniques.

With a shrug, she decided to check her phone for distractions, hoping Marty wouldn't be too far behind. As she scrolled through the usual flurry of updates, a post from the self-proclaimed fitness guru, Jess Thompson, caught her eye.

The name elicited a groan. Jess was a local fitness trainer and Instagram influencer whose social media presence bordered on the obnoxious. Her perfectly posed pictures and self-satisfied captions touting the superiority of her particular brand of exercise grated on Jamie's nerves, even if Jess Thompson did always look stunning and in enviable shape. Every squat thrust and burpee seemed to be accompanied by a thinly veiled jab at anyone who dared to get their sweat on in a different way.

Jess had posted a video of her training some people who were hurling over huge tractor tires. The caption read something along the lines of *this is the only way to get in shape & yoga is for losers.*

Jamie rolled her eyes. Jess was a talented trainer, no doubt, but her constant need to put down other forms of exercise rubbed Jamie the wrong way.

Jess looked beautiful, her glossy chestnut hair in a neat bun. Her elegant, perfectly muscled frame was provocatively dressed in skin tight yoga pants and a tiny crop top that barely covered her breasts.

Jamie caught herself scrolling Jess's photos. Something about Jess's piercing blue eyes and full sensual lips was so attractive.

Stop looking, Jamie. That is what she wants you to feel. She wants you to want her.

Ignoring the urge to unleash a scathing comment, Jamie hit the "See Less Of" button, effectively banishing Jess' smug persona from her feed.

A few messages from clients, friends, and family elicited quick replies, and with a final sigh, she tucked the phone away to continue her attempts at fishing.

She took in the gentle lapping of waves against the shore and the chirping of crickets in the tall grass. A glance at her watch told her Marty should be arriving any minute. Maybe his arrival would break the fish's apparent disinterest, hopefully.

"Hey there, stranger! Looks like the fish are hiding from you today."

Marty's footsteps announced him on the creaky floorboards, a wide grin on his face. A tackle box was slung over one shoulder and a cooler—the unmistakable promise of ice-cold beers—in the other hand completed the picture of a perfect fishing buddy.

Despite sharing Jamie's height, he favored a more generous build, the result of questionable junk foods. A faded green fishing hat sat perched on his head, casting a shadow over his perpetually sun-kissed cheeks. Wearing a fishing vest, his green eyes sparkled with mischief as he got closer.

"Marty! About time. Took you long enough."

He greeted Jamie with a peck on the cheek and sat next to her on the dock.

"Whoa, new look, Marty?" His sandy blonde hair, which used to be a perpetually windblown mess, was now neatly trimmed, adding a touch of distinguished charm.

He chuckled, running a hand self-consciously through his shorter hair. "Wife finally decided it was time for a change. Said I was starting to look like a lost member of The Beatles."

Jamie burst out laughing. "Hey, there's nothing

wrong with a little mop-top charm! But yeah, this definitely suits you better. You look... distinguished."

Marty raised an eyebrow, a playful smirk tugging at the corners of his mouth. "Distinguished, huh? Not sure that's the word Laura used, but I'll take it."

"Well, you definitely pull off the *responsible husband* vibe now."

They laughed.

"So, what took you so long? Traffic?"

Marty chuckled. "Traffic? Here? In the middle of nowhere? Nah, little bump tried to make an appearance this morning. Seems the little one is impatient to greet the world."

Her eyes widened in surprise. "Wait, what? Are you serious?"

He nodded. "Yep, false alarm this morning. But the doctor says it won't be long now. Maybe a week, two at the most."

"Oh my, Marty, that's amazing! I can't believe it's happening so soon."

The prospect of Marty becoming a father was both daunting and exhilarating. He'd always been the fun-loving, carefree one, and fatherhood would undoubtedly be a life-changing adventure.

"You ready for it, buddy?" she asked.

"Ready as I'll ever be. A little scared, sure. But mostly excited. Can't wait to meet the little one."

He popped the cooler open, revealing a frosty wonderland of perfectly chilled beers.

"Alright, enough chit-chat. Time to quench our thirst and then maybe tempt those elusive fish with a little offering."

Marty took a swig of his beer, discerning my features. "You alright, Jamie? You seem a bit... distant today."

He'd always been that way—uncanny at picking up on the tiniest shifts in her mood.

"Yeah, I'm fine. Just broke up with Amy," Jamie replied and offered a weak smile.

"The MIA girlfriend? Finally! You know, I've always told you to move on from her."

"Yeah, I know. You were right. It just took me a while to see it myself."

"Sounds like you needed to. You deserve better than someone who gives you the silent treatment."

"Yeah, well, better late than never, right?"

"Yeah," he said, raising his bottle in a silent

toast. "Listen, take some time for yourself. You deserve a break from the whole dating scene."

"That's what I was thinking too. Maybe a good long break. I need to rediscover myself and learn to spot those toxic traits before I get sucked in again."

"Smart move. You know you're worth more than someone who can't even bother to show up for a date, right?"

She sighed, taking a long drink from her beer. "Honestly, I think I'm just not lucky in relationships."

Marty offered a reassuring smile. "You're awesome, Jamie. You'll find the right woman soon enough. Just keep your eyes peeled and don't settle for anything less than amazing."

"Besides, the dating pool is full of fish. You're bound to find the right one eventually," he continued.

She laughed, nudging him playfully. "This isn't one of your therapy sessions, Marty."

"Since when have I not been your therapist? Ever since college, you've been dumping your relationship woes on me."

"Alright, Dr. Marty, give me some more words of wisdom," she teased.

He leaned back against the log, a thoughtful

look on his face. "Look, Jamie, you're strong, independent, and you've got a bigger heart than anyone I know. You're basically Wonder Woman but with a fishing rod."

She smiled. "Okay, that's a new one."

He chuckled. "But seriously," his voice became low and serious, "there's something else you might not know. I... I used to have feelings for you. More than just friends."

Her breath caught. That was completely unexpected.

"But," he added quickly, holding up a hand, "when I saw you weren't interested, that you liked girls... Well, I just buried those feelings. Figured it wasn't fair to either of us. And I got over it and found a woman who makes me happy."

"Marty... I-I had no idea."

He smiled gently. "It's okay. I didn't want you to know. All that matters now is you find someone who's deserving of you, like I did. Someone who appreciates your strength, your kindness, and your killer fishing skills."

They sat in comfortable silence for a moment, the only sound the chirping of crickets and the distant call of a loon.

"Speaking of which, the client you sent my way

for yoga? He's doing fantastic. Says his anxiety has improved tremendously," Jamie said in an attempt at changing the subject.

Marty's face lit up. "That's great news! Mental health is no joke, you know. Glad I could connect you two."

Suddenly, Marty's rod jerked violently, pulling him forward in a surprised yelp.

"Aha! Looks like someone finally decided to join the party!" he shouted with a laugh, as the fishing rod bent with surprising resistance.

A frantic battle ensued, with him expertly maneuvering the rod as the unseen creature fought back.

Jamie let out a whoop of delight, clapping her hands together. "There you go, Marty! I knew you wouldn't let me down."

She was relieved not just for the fish but for the shift in the emotional tide.

Finally, with a triumphant flourish, he hauled a glistening bass onto the bank.

"There you are, you little rascal!" he exclaimed, holding the fish up proudly.

They laughed as Marty expertly removed the hook and prepared to clean the fish.

"So," Marty said, wiping his hands on his

pants, "Let's head back to my place? Laura would love to see you after all this time. We can throw this guy on the grill and catch up properly."

The idea of some delicious grilled fish and Laura's warm company was also undeniably appealing.

"That sounds great, Marty. Thanks."

"Excellent! Let's get this fish cleaned up then. Laura's a whiz with marinades, you're in for a treat."

6

JESS

Grocery weekend. Jess' fridge was officially a wasteland—land of the wilted lettuce and questionable cheese chunks.

Ugh, the grocery store was a jungle on Saturdays, but she was able to fight through the crowd. Basket in hand, she weaved through the produce section, dodging rogue elbows and mentally ticking off the list. Eggs, milk, bread—the holy trinity of any respectable fridge. She grabbed some frozen veggies, then headed towards the hygiene section.

Her skin had been freaking out lately, so she needed a new moisturizer. There were a million options, all with names that sounded like they belonged in a spaceship.

Just as she was about to grab a random bottle with vaguely appealing packaging, a voice cut through her internal debate.

"Ooh, that one's not bad, but have you tried this?" She looked up to see a woman holding a different bottle, a familiar smile plastered on her face.

Wait. Was that...? No way. Of course it was Sam. Her ex. Here. In the moisturizer aisle. Couldn't she have just picked another grocery store? Another planet?

Sam smiled hesitantly. "I've been using this one for months and my skin loves it." She held up the bottle for Jess' inspection.

Great. Just what she needed. Moisturizer advice from the woman who broke her heart two years ago.

"Thanks, but I think I'll stick with this one," Jess mumbled, grabbing the bottle she was originally eyeing.

"Jess, hold on a sec," Sam said, reaching out and grabbing her wrist.

Her grip was surprisingly gentle, compared to

the way she ripped their relationship apart with a cold, "I just don't love you anymore" two years ago.

"Uh, can I help you with something?" Jess forced a smile, her voice tight.

"Can we just talk for a minute?"

"Shoot."

"I just wanted to apologize."

Jess scoffed, the sound sharp and dismissive. "Apologize? For what, Sam? For falling out of love? Newsflash, that's a pretty good reason to break up with someone, wouldn't you say?"

"No, that's not..." Sam stammered, searching for the right words. "I... I shouldn't have said that. It was a terrible excuse."

"Maybe so. But the damage is done, isn't it?" Jess said, her voice devoid of emotion.

She was reminded of the time she spent piecing her shattered heart back together while Sam... Well, who knows what Sam was doing.

Truth be told, it had taken a while to get there. Months of sleepless nights, tear-stained pillows, and the suffocating weight of a love that felt so one-sided. Even the mere mention of Sam's name could bring tears to her eyes. Every song, every movie, every shared memory felt like a fresh stab wound.

She replayed every conversation, every argument in her head, searching for some clue, some missed opportunity to fix things. But there was nothing. Sam simply fell out of love.

She'd poured everything she had into that relationship, always available, always willing to bend over backwards to make it work. But in the end, it wasn't enough.

There was a part of her, a tiny, bruised part, that still wondered if it was something she did. Was she not attentive enough? Too clingy? But logic drowned out the whispers of doubt. Love, real love, shouldn't be this easy to walk away from.

"Jess, I..." Sam started again, but she cut her off with a gentle shake of her head.

"Honestly, you don't need to say sorry. I've already moved on."

She excused herself with a polite nod, maneuvering around Sam's cart and heading towards the checkout.

As she reached the front of the line, she stole a glance back. Sam was still standing there, a lost look on her face. Maybe a part of her regretted letting Jess go, but that was a bridge she burned down a long time ago.

Seeing her today was a confirmation. She'd moved on. Her life was full; her career was thriving, her apartment felt like a haven, and having a relationship was ruled out entirely.

Maybe someday she'd open herself up again, but for now, she was perfectly content being alone.

Scrolling through her social media feed, Jess' perfectly manicured finger paused over a post titled, "Yoga for Everyone: 5 Simple Poses to De-Stress."

The accompanying picture showed a woman, Jamie Nguyen, in a downward-facing dog pose, a basic, beginner move. Jamie Nguyen looked tall and all lean muscles and ridiculously flexible. She had dark glossy hair and big grey eyes.

Jess scoffed. Sure, that all sounded lovely, but where was the challenge? Where was the push that forced you to confront your physical limitations and emerge stronger on the other side?

These "gentle flow" yoga routines were all well and good, but for her, the real magic happened when she was digging deep, muscles burning, sweat dripping—that's when she found true mental and physical resilience.

A mischievous glint crept into her eyes. Jamie Nguyen, huh? Sounds like someone needed a good dose of reality. This might ruffle some feathers, but a little controversy was practically her middle name. After all, if it wasn't generating a buzz, was it even Jess Thompson?

Tapping on the post, she read through Jamie's spiel about the benefits of gentle yoga for stress relief and overall well-being. It was all fluffy language and basic stretches—nothing that would get your heart rate up or leave you feeling truly accomplished.

She crafted her comment.

Simple? More like snooze-ville. If you're serious about results, skip the downward-facing dogs and get yourself to a proper boot camp class. Sweat, strain, feel the burn – that's what gets you toned and stress-free, not holding a pose for 30 seconds.

Adding a fire emoji for effect, she hit *post*, a thrill of anticipation coursing through her.

This was bound to stir the pot. People craved a little debate, and Jess Thompson was always happy to provide it.

Her phone buzzed with Jamie's reply.

Jess, intensity is great, but it's not everything. You wouldn't expect to build a house with just a hammer, would you? Yoga builds the foundation - strength, flexibility, focus - that allows you to push yourself even harder in other workouts.

Okay, that metaphor was actually kind of good. But she wasn't about to let her have the upper hand.

Maybe not, but you wouldn't get very far just laying the foundation either, would you? Sometimes you gotta put on the hard hat and get to work!

The comments were lighting up faster than she could refresh the page. One user chimed in, seemingly on Jamie's side:

Preach, Jamie! Yoga isn't just about stretching – it's built mental grit too. I used to get winded walking up the stairs, but after a month of yoga, I hiked a whole mountain! Strength comes in many forms.

Another user threw their support behind her:

Jess is right though! My friend went from barely being able to do a pushup to crushing her first Spartan Race after joining boot camp. You gotta push yourself to see real change!

The argument kept going for hours nonstop.

Who is this bloody Jamie Nguyen anyway?

The insistent ring of the doorbell cut through the apartment. Groaning internally, Jess pushed herself away from the computer, expecting the usual delivery guy, probably standing there with the boots she ordered.

Instead, a familiar face broke into a wide grin, framed by a mess of wild red curls that accentuated their sharp cheekbones. They were rocking a band t-shirt and ripped jeans, the very image of effortless cool.

"Hey girl! How's the queen of boot camp been ruling the fitness world?"

"Isa!" Jess shouted, throwing her arms open in surprise.

Her childhood best friend, Isabel, stood on the doorstep, their backpack slung over one shoulder, a mischievous glint in their hazel eyes.

"What are you doing here? I thought you were in Mexico for another month?"

Isabel, non-binary and fiercely proud of it, threw their head back and laughed.

"Surprise!" they said, pulling Jess into a tight hug. "Turns out, Mexico got a little too... relaxing. I needed some real Jess energy in my life."

Here, in front of her, stood the person who'd known her since scraped knees and trading Lisa Frank stickers, the one who'd patiently listened to her rant about boys (and now, maybe, fitness instructors) for hours on end.

"Come on in," Jess said, pulling Isa inside and shutting the door behind them. "Let me get you some water, and then you need to tell me *everything* about your trip."

Pushing open the fridge, Jess scanned the shelves, bypassing the sparkling water in favor of two cold beers.

Isa flopped down on the couch, flinging their backpack onto the floor with a dramatic sigh.

"Here you go," Jess said, handing them a bottle. "Local IPA, perfect for rehydration after a Mexican adventure."

Isa took a long swig, letting out a satisfied sigh. "Mmm, that hits the spot. So, what's all this I hear about you stirring up trouble online?" they asked, a playful glint in their eyes.

Jess knew this wouldn't stay a secret long. Isa

always had a nose for drama, even from miles away.

She grinned. "You know me too well," she said, taking a long swig. Briefly, she explained the back-and-forth with Jamie bloody Nguyen, the yoga instructor practically living rent-free in her head.

There was something about Jamie that drew her in and pissed her off all at once.

"Jess, you instigator! You know you could have just scrolled past her post, right?"

"But where's the fun in that? Besides, someone needs to stand up for the glorious world of boot camp sweating!"

Isa took a thoughtful sip of their beer, then grinned. "Okay, okay, I get it. But seriously, can't there be room for both yoga and boot camp in the fitness world?"

"Who cares?"

"Maybe you can challenge Jamie to a fitness fusion class—half yoga, half boot camp. Winner gets bragging rights for a month!"

The idea sparked a fire in Jess, both hilarious and oddly compelling. "You know what, that might just be the perfect way to end this whole thing."

They both laughed.

"But seriously though, why don't you just stay

out of it? Yoga, boot camp, who cares? People can choose what works for them."

Jess smirked. "Yeah, you're probably right. Besides, I'd rather be catching up with my favorite travel buddy than arguing with some internet stranger about downward-facing dogs."

Suddenly, Isa reached into their backpack and pulled out a small, brightly colored package.

"I brought you a little something from Mexico."

Jess took the package. Isa always knew how to make her feel special. "You shouldn't have," she said, carefully unwrapping the paper. Inside sat a beautiful silver necklace with a tiny cactus pendant.

"For the toughest trainer this side of the equator. Besides, it reminded me of you—strong, resilient, and thrives in the heat." Isa said with a wink.

Tears welled up in Jess' eyes. "Isa, you're the best," she managed to choke out, pulling them into a tight hug.

"De nada. You don't need to thank me."

Finally, Jess pulled back, wiping her eyes. "So, how are things with your folks? Did they come around to the whole, you know, not-a-girl-not-a-boy thing?"

Isa's smile faltered for a brief moment. "They're trying. There's still a lot of... confusion, on their part. But hey, at least they're not disowning me anymore. Besides, I'm not holding my breath for a Pride Parade invitation anytime soon, but baby steps, I guess."

Jess squeezed their hand sympathetically. "That's good. Change can be hard, especially for older generations.

"How about your mom? And Riley?"

"Mom's good. She actually loved the scarf you sent for her birthday. Said it was perfect for those chilly evenings. And Riley loves those video games."

They chatted for a while longer, catching up on everything from Isa's adventures in Mexico to the latest gossip with their old friends. Finally, Isa yawned widely.

"Whoa, traveling home has caught up to me," they said, stretching their legs. "Maybe I should hit the hay."

"Yeah, probably," Jess agreed, glancing at the clock. It was later than she realized.

She walked Isa to the spare bedroom, making sure they had fresh towels and everything they needed.

"Hey," Jess said as Isa was about to close the door.

"Yeah?" Isa asked, leaning against the doorframe.

"How about tomorrow, we hit the gym together? You can be the judge of who has the better workout, yoga or boot camp."

Isa's eyes lit up with a familiar challenge. "You're on," they said with a grin.

Just as Jess stepped out of the room, her phone chimed, revealing an email. Her eyes widened in surprise.

"Whoa!"

"What is it?" Isa came running.

With trembling fingers, Jess showed them the email.

The subject line screamed at her in bold letters:

Subject: Ultimate Body Battle: Interview Invitation

Dear Jessica Thompson,

We'd like to invite you to interview for a spot as a trainer on the upcoming season of Ultimate Body Battle!

The interview will be held on Tuesday, May 14th at 10:00 AM at our Los Angeles studios. During the inter-

view, you'll have the opportunity to meet with our
production team and discuss your training philosophy
and experience.

We're excited to learn more about you!
Sincerely,
The Ultimate Body Battle Team

"Holy Moly!" Jess breathed, a mixture of shock and exhilaration coursing through her.

Isa snatched the phone from her hand, their eyes scanning the email with amusement.

"Well, well, well. Look who stirred up a little too much trouble online. Seems like your internet brawl caught the right attention," they said with a smile.

"You think this is because of that whole yoga-versus-boot-camp thing?"

"Bingo!" Isa said, snapping their fingers. "Did you think that after stirring up all that trouble online, you wouldn't get noticed? Looks like your troublemaking has paid off, Jess! You totally deserve to be on that show."

Excitement bubbled in Jess' chest, threatening to overflow. "I know, right?" she said, grabbing Isa in a spontaneous hug. "This is huge! This is a big reality tv show! Drinks are definitely on me. How about we head over to the bar? My treat to celebrate... and maybe strategize for this interview?"

Isa raised an eyebrow playfully. "Strategize, huh? Sounds like you're already planning to win."

"Well, someone's gotta bring the heat."

They laughed.

7

JAMIE

Stepping out of her car, Jamie stretched luxuriously, feeling the satisfying pops in her lower back after a killer yoga session.

As she headed towards her apartment building, Mr. Fred, her ever-cheerful neighbor from across the street, waved her over with his trusty lawnmower.

Gotta hand it to the guy, at 75, he still kept his lawn looking like a putting green. His shock of white hair, as wild as a windblown dandelion, framed a wrinkled face that spoke of a life well-lived.

His lanky build belied surprising strength, evident in the way he maneuvered the heavy lawnmower with practiced ease. Weathered skin, thanks to years spent outdoors, crinkled around his eyes as he smiled.

A faded baseball cap, perched precariously on his head, cast a shadow over his twinkling blue eyes. His clothes, a mismatched assortment of worn jeans and a paint-splattered T-shirt, spoke of a life less concerned with fashion and more focused on getting the job done.

"Morning, Jamie! Saw that little dust-up you had online with that boot camp trainer yesterday. Quite a show, that was!"

Her stomach clenched. Jess Thompson. The name itself sent a jolt of irritation through her. Honestly, who did she think she was? Couldn't she just stick to her barbells and burpees without trying to discredit the power of yoga? Sure, a good sweat session had its place, but there was so much more to fitness than just physical exertion.

Mr. Fred seemed oblivious to her internal grumbling. "But hey, all that attention can't be bad for business, right?" He winked, clearly enjoying the spectacle.

Easy for him to say. He was on the sidelines, watching the popcorn fly.

She forced a smile. "Oh, you saw that?"

"Sure did!" Mr. Fred beamed. "Keeps things interesting, doesn't it?"

But she hated to admit Mr. Fred might be right. Thanks to their online tirade, her post about the benefits of yoga versus Jess' barbaric boot camp torture sessions had *exploded*. Over two million views on TikTok! Two million! She couldn't believe it!

Seems there was a silver lining to all this. A little online sparring might be exactly what her business needed. After all, any publicity was good publicity, right?

"You got that right," she said, her voice a little tighter than she'd like.

Perhaps she could use this newfound attention to spread the message of yoga's benefits further than ever before.

Jess Thompson might have started the fire, but she could use it to illuminate the path to inner peace—for everyone, even boot camp-loving bullies like her.

Stepping inside with a sigh, the air conditioning instantly washed away the morning heat.

Just as she reached for her water bottle, a notification chimed on her phone.

She unlocked the screen, hoping it was nothing else about the online brawl, and her eyes widened in surprise.

"Ultimate Body Battle?" she said out loud in confusion. This couldn't be real. Could it?

Tapping on the notification, she was greeted with an email subject line that made her heart skip a beat:

Ultimate Body Battle: Interview Invitation.

Her stomach erupted in a flurry of butterflies. No way!

She quickly scanned the email, each word confirming her wildest dream. The producers of Ultimate Body Battle, the very same show she spent countless evenings curled up on the couch watching, wanted to interview her, Jamie Nguyen, for a spot as a trainer on their upcoming season!

A joyous squeal escaped her lips before she could contain it. Doing a little happy dance in her living room might seem silly, but right now, she didn't care. This was incredible!

The email detailed the interview date, time, and location—a studio there in Los Angeles.

The thought of guiding a team through physical and mental challenges, of sharing her passion for yoga with a wider audience, sent a thrill coursing through her. This could be a game-changer for her career.

Suddenly, the Jess Thompson situation paled in comparison. Who cared about a petty online fight when this kind of opportunity came knocking? Ultimate Body Battle. Her. A chance to truly inspire people and show them the transformative power of yoga.

A wide grin split her face as she reread the email. It was time to take her practice—and her message—to a whole new level.

Pulling her Mazda into a parking spot outside the imposing glass and steel complex housing the Ultimate Body Battle studios, Jamie straightened her pantsuit and took a deep, centering breath.

Today was the day. Just as she was about to step away from her car, she noticed a silver SUV gleaming under the harsh sunlight, parked right next to her. And like some kind of cosmic joke, Jess Thompson was just getting out of it. She must have been invited for the interview as well. Damn it.

There she was, preening like a beautiful blue eyed peacock in her window. Their eyes locked for a beat, tension crackling between them thicker than the smog hanging over the city.

Neither made a move to greet the other. In fact, a silent competition seemed to erupt—who could appear the most nonchalant? Then, just as quickly, Jess looked away, pretending Jamie wasn't there.

As far as Jamie was concerned, Jess was a ghost, a figment of her recent online past. She was here for an interview, and that was her sole focus. But even as she marched towards the imposing glass doors, she couldn't help but replay Jess' features.

The Jess Thompson of the internet, the one spewing fire and brimstone about the superiority of boot camp, was one thing. But the Jess Thompson she just saw in person? She was a goddess.

She might be the competition, but Jamie had to admit, Jess looked even more impressive in person. Her pictures online didn't do her justice. Tall and statuesque, with a lean, muscular build that spoke volumes about her dedication to fitness.

Even in a simple T-shirt and ripped jeans, she exuded an aura of raw power and confidence. Her sun-kissed skin glowed, highlighting her flawless complexion, and she had a combination of strength and grace that was oddly captivating—different from the aggressive persona she projected online.

A traitorous part of Jamie, a part she quickly shoved back down, was even a little curious. What was Jess Thompson really like? Was the online persona just a carefully crafted image, or was there more to her?

Ugh, Jamie, focus! This was a professional interview, not a beauty pageant.

Jess might be a walking advertisement for human potential, but Jamie had her own strengths to offer. Her passion, her knowledge, her ability to connect with people on a deeper level.

Pushing those thoughts aside with a determined shake of her head, she squared her shoulders and entered the cool, air-conditioned lobby.

The Ultimate Body Battle interview awaited, and she was ready to show them exactly why she deserved to be a trainer on their show.

Pushing open the studio doors, Jamie was greeted by a wave of nervous energy.

Glancing at the clock on the wall, she cursed under her breath. Her interview wasn't for another hour, but the other nine participants seemed to be there already, in the waiting area.

The friendly receptionist, a woman with a nametag that read *Angela* in a cheerful script, flashed a smile. Her short, blonde hair was neatly styled in a bob that framed her face, which seemed permanently set in a look of warm welcome. Her outfit was the picture of professional courtesy—a crisp black blazer hung over a knee-length skirt in a shade of teal that perfectly matched the company logo pinned to her lapel.

She pointed towards the only empty spot left in the waiting room, and Jamie's smile faltered slightly as she noticed the one detail that could potentially disrupt her calm.

The only empty spot left was right next to Jess Thompson.

There she was; the very picture of nonchalance. While everyone else was sporting interview-ready power suits or crisp blouses, she stuck out like a sore thumb in her casuals that screamed *Weekend Hike*. Not to mention the oversized headphones practically welded to her ears, blocking out the world.

Did she seriously think this was a gym session? Jamie narrowed her eyes at her. She couldn't miss Jamie's skeptical stare, but she pretended not to notice, a barely-there smirk playing on her lips. Did she...enjoy this little forced proximity?

Jess continued to bob her head to the music, as Jamie plopped herself down with a sigh. But the bass pulsing from Jess' headphones was a constant, unwelcome presence.

Ugh. The urge to rip off her headphones and launch into a lecture about interview etiquette was strong. But professionalism won out.

Focus, Jamie. Maintain a healthy distance from this walking negativity.

But the music, a relentless electronic beat, kept worming its way into Jamie's concentration. A silent battle of wills ensued.

Jamie glared at Jess pointedly, hoping she'd get the hint. Jess, in turn, pretended to be utterly oblivious, her gaze fixed on her phone.

Finally, after what felt like an eternity, Jess glanced up, with a devilish smirk. The silence between them was thick with unspoken animosity like two storm clouds.

They were both well aware of the online battle that brought them here, and the unspoken subtext hung heavy: *Can you believe we both ended up here?*

The message was clear; this interview waiting room had just become a battleground of passive aggression.

Jamie looked away and decided to channel her inner yogi, with a book she pulled out from her bag.

One by one, the hopeful trainers disappeared behind the frosted glass doors of the interview room, only to emerge moments later with varying expressions on their faces. Finally, the receptionist called Jamie Nguyen's name.

Taking a deep breath, Jamie rose from the chair, her gaze flicking briefly towards Jess, who offered a sardonic salute with two fingers. Ignoring the urge to roll her eyes, Jamie straightened her clothes and headed towards the glass doors leading to the interview room.

The room was bright and furnished with a

polished wooden table and three comfortable chairs.

The interview room offered a sense of neutral professionalism. Bright lighting ensured everyone could see each other clearly, while a polished wooden table and three comfortable chairs provided a functional space for conversation. It was uncluttered and professional, designed to put interviewees at ease without offering any distractions.

Two men and a woman sat behind the table, looking professional in their suits.

"Jamie Nguyen?" the woman in the center asked, a warm smile softening her features. "Please, come in and have a seat."

She was a vision of professional elegance. Her sharp, shoulder-length blonde bob framed a face that seemed both youthful and authoritative.

A well-tailored black suit hugged her curves, the crisp white blouse beneath the blazer hinting at a hint of personality peeking through the polished exterior. A swipe of classic red lipstick added a touch of vibrancy, completing the picture of a woman who meant business but with a disarming warmth.

Jamie nodded, taking the offered chair in the middle. "Thank you for having me."

"The pleasure is all ours," the man on the right said. "I'm Wills, and these are my colleagues, Sophia and Terry. We're the producers of Ultimate Body Battle."

The man was elegantly dressed in his tailored charcoal suit. His black hair was neatly cropped, not a strand out of place. A crisp white shirt peeked out from under the vest, and a colorful silk tie added a touch of personality to his otherwise conservative attire.

"Alright, Ms. Nguyen, tell us about your experience as a yoga instructor. How long have you been teaching?" Wills asked.

"I've been teaching yoga for eight years now, but my passion for it goes back much further than that. Yoga helped me reconnect with my body and mind after a difficult time in my life, and I'm dedicated to sharing its transformative power with others."

"Can you elaborate on that a bit? What sets your approach to yoga apart?" Sophia asked.

"For me, yoga isn't just about physical postures. It's about creating a sense of balance and well-being in all aspects of life. I believe in tailoring my approach to each individual, helping them find their own inner strength and resilience."

"Interesting," Terry muttered, stroking his chin thoughtfully. "And how would you translate that philosophy to working with a team on Ultimate Body Battle? The show is known for its intensity and competitive spirit."

Terry was a picture of corporate composure, with his brown hair meticulously styled in a side part. The crisp lines of his charcoal suit hinted at a man who valued order and control.

A smile spread across Jamie's face. "Challenges can be a powerful motivator. On Ultimate Body Battle, I wouldn't just be pushing my team physically. I'd be there to support them mentally and emotionally, helping them overcome obstacles and discover their hidden potential."

Wills raised an eyebrow. "Interesting. Many of our trainers here at Ultimate Body Battle come from a more traditional fitness background. What makes yoga a unique and effective approach to achieving results?"

"Yoga incorporates breathwork, mindfulness, and mental focus to create a holistic approach to well-being. It's not just about building muscle or burning calories; it's about building resilience, improving flexibility, and fostering a sense of inner peace. These are all qualities that can contribute to a person's overall success, both on the show and in their daily lives."

"What kind of yoga do you specialize in?" Sophia inquired, leaning forward with interest.

"I primarily teach Vinyasa flow, but I also incorporate elements of Hatha and restorative yoga into my classes, depending on the needs of my students."

The conversation flowed easily, and Jamie could tell the producers were engaged. Then, just as they were wrapping up the standard interview questions, Terry leaned forward with a smirk.

"We've been very impressed with your work. Like the other participants, we did some research and were particularly struck by your passion for yoga and the positive impact you have on your clients."

"But, what really caught our eye was your recent TikTok post," Sophia added.

Jamie's breath hitched. The post. The one where she (perhaps a little too vehemently) defended yoga against Jess' boot camp claims.

"Oh, right. That was... quite the discussion," Jamie said, trying to sound nonchalant.

Wills chuckled. "Let's just say it generated a lot of buzz. And that's one of the qualities we look for in our trainers—the ability to spark conversation, to get people excited about fitness. We want trainers who are passionate, not afraid to stand up for what they believe in."

Jamie was relieved. So, the online brawl with Jess wasn't negative after all? In fact, it might have even helped her case!

8

JESS

Her head held high, Jess sashayed out of the interview room, the positive vibes practically radiating from her. Nailing that interview felt like conquering Mount Everest in Lululemons. Just another day in the life of Jess Thompson, future Ultimate Body Battle champion, that's her!

With a pep in her step, she headed towards the restroom, needing to freshen up before heading home.

Pushing open the ladies' room door, she was greeted by the sight of Jamie bloody Nguyen's elegant back bent over the sink. Ugh. Great.

Just what she needed, another reminder of the online brawl and that infuriating sneer painted on

Jamie's face. Jess clenched her jaw, ready to make a beeline for a stall and get out of there as quickly as possible.

But then, Jamie straightened up as she washed her hands, and for a moment, Jess forgot everything else. It was like a strange feeling sneaked up on her. It wasn't animosity or irritation; it was something closer to... attraction?

Jess didn't often find women who matched her height and stature and although Jamie seemed somehow more graceful leaner and long limbed, Jess enjoyed running her gaze over Jamie's body. Jamie looked like a more masculine version of Jess. She didn't have the full breasts or thick eyelashes Jess had. Jamie had a strong jawline and lovely wide set brown eyes, and very sexy muscular shoulders.

High cheekbones, full lips curved into a soft smile, and eyes the color of melted chocolate. Maybe it was that her figure filled out her pantsuit in a way that was both graceful and powerful. Whatever it was, Jess found herself completely caught off guard by this sudden shift in perspective.

Okay, Jess, focus. This is not the time to be appreciating the enemy's perfectly sculpted silhouette. There's no time for impromptu lesbian crushes in the bathroom. Besides, you're a boot camp queen, not some love-struck yoga enthusiast. Just get in, get out, and maintain your aura of intimidating confidence.

But seriously, Jamie was like a walking fitness magazine cover come to life. Thick, toned, with a healthy glow that screamed yoga master. It was almost enough to make Jess reconsider her entire boot-camp-or-bust philosophy. Almost.

Suddenly, Jamie turned, and their eyes met, and for a split second, Jess was frozen. Did Jamie catch her staring? There was no way she could let her know she was practically checking her out.

Trying to mask her surprise, Jess forced a smirk and headed towards the sink next to Jamie. Turning on the faucet, she lathered her hands with soap, hoping to appear nonchalant.

They finished washing their hands at the same time and reached for the air dryer simultaneously, their bodies momentarily blocking each other's path.

"Excuse me," Jess muttered, trying to sound polite but failing miserably.

Jamie stepped back slightly, her lips twitching at the corners. "Oh, go ahead," she said, her voice surprisingly gentle.

Before Jess could even process this turn of events, Jamie stepped aside with a smile. Jess mumbled a quick thanks and blasted her hands with hot air, trying to ignore the sudden warmth spreading through her chest.

This was so bizarre. One minute she was ready to rip Jamie's head off for her online antics, the next she was... flustered? By Jamie Nguyen?

Her mind short-circuited. Was Jamie flirting with her? Was this some elaborate Zen mind trick? What was happening here? This wasn't how this was supposed to go!

They were supposed to be bitter rivals, locked in a battle for fitness supremacy and social media dominance. But that smile... damn, that smile was messing with her in ways she couldn't explain.

Jess watched with forced nonchalance as Jamie used the air dryer furthest from her. The yoga instructor seemed to practically glow with post-interview satisfaction.

This unexpected bathroom encounter was turning out to be strangely entertaining. Maybe the pre-interview jitters had fried her brain a little, because there was no denying the undeniable pull she felt towards Jamie. It was insane.

Just as Jamie reached for the bathroom door,

Jess spotted a white handkerchief peeking out from the counter next to the sink.

"Hey!" she called out, her voice sharper than intended. Jamie whirled around, surprised.

"Uh, you left that," Jess said, gesturing to the handkerchief.

"Oh! Thank you," Jamie stammered, approaching the counter at the same time as Jess.

Both women reached for the handkerchief, their hands brushing in the process. Their eyes locked, and for a breathless second, the air crackled with something other than competitive tension.

An inexplicable urge flowed through Jess, a strong pull that defied logic or reason.

Jamie, cheeks flushed and eyes wide, mumbled a flustered, "Thank you," before turning towards the door.

But as she reached for the handle, a voice inside her seemed to speak up. She glanced back at Jess, whose eyes were fixed on her with burning desire.

Before either of them could fully comprehend what was happening, they were lunging towards each other again. They met halfway, lips colliding in a kiss that was anything but peaceful.

It was fierce, urgent, a clash of wills that somehow morphed into something more. Jess, the queen of control, found herself lost in the unexpected heat. She wasn't sure what came over her. Maybe it was the lingering scent of lavender soap clinging to Jamie's hand, or the vulnerability in her surprised eyes. Whatever it was, it was a force she couldn't resist.

Jamie, for her part, melted into the kiss, her initial fluster giving way to a surprised gasp that quickly dissolved into a shaky moan. Her hands, which had been clutching the counter for support, found their way around Jess' back, pulling her closer.

The kiss was unlike anything they had ever experienced, a potent mix of rivalry and... something else entirely.

Jess felt a flutter deep inside, a thrill that made her want to explore this woman's body. The idea of doing something so naughty in such a formal place made her excitement skyrocket.

Without hesitation, Jamie guided Jess into the doggy style position bent forward in front of the mirror, pulling down her pants and underwear to reveal her ass. Jess found herself fully compliant-

although it felt crazy in a public bathroom where anyone could walk in on them.

It felt like forever since Jess had had any sex that truly excited her. And right here, in a public place, with her pants pulled down exposing her to Jamie Nguyen, this felt truly exciting. She could feel herself getting wet.

Starting gently, Jamie teased Jess' clitoris with her fingers sliding easily through Jess's wetness. Her touch made Jess try to hold back her moans.

"Doing it my way, now, aren't you, Thompson?" Jamie's left hand adjusted Jess's chin upwards so they were both looking at their joint reflection in the bathroom mirror while her right hand teased Jess's wet pussy. She could see her own embarrassed and vulnerable blue eyes next to Jamie's firm and downright sexy brown eyes. Jamie's eyes looked hungry for her and Jess felt like putty in her hands.

Jess nodded as Jamie continued to slide her fingers around between Jess's legs, almost casually, teasingly.

Jess felt herself moaning, she couldn't help it. This was such a turn on!

"Those are cute little whimpers, Thompson.

Anyone would think you want me to fuck you. Is that what you want?"

No!

Jamie's gaze was hungry in the mirror and Jess was so turned on. She nodded again.

Jamie's fingers suddenly pulled away. "Say the words, Thompson. I want you to beg me to fuck you, or I'll leave you here, wet and wanting with your panties round your ankles."

Jess saw her own eyes widen.

Fuck. How on earth have I ended up here?

Jess knew she should have played it a lot cooler a lot earlier. Because unfortunately now she was way too turned on to turn back.

"Please..." she heard herself whisper.

"Please, what?"

"Please, fuck me..."

With that, she felt Jamie's fingers plunge deep inside her and she called out, loudly, her body thrown forward.

"Oh, my god!"

Closing her eyes, Jess surrendered to the wave of sensations crashing over her.

"Keep your eyes open." She felt Jamie grabbing her chin again and forcing her to look in the mirror. "I want to see your eyes submit to me when you come."

Her lips parted in a silent gasp, trying to contain the moans threatening to escape as she looked into the mirror- her own eyes and Jamie's. With each forceful thrust of Jamie's fingers curled against her G spot, she felt herself teetering on the edge. She bit down on her lip, desperate to keep from crying out. But it was a losing battle. Her body betrayed her, arching into the exquisite torture, begging for release.

The forbidden thrill of doing this in a formal space, and the fact that they could be caught, added an electrifying edge to the experience. Her body moved in rhythm with Jamie's movements, feeling the tension coil tighter and tighter within her.

She couldn't hold back any longer. With a surge, she exploded, squirting hot and long right down her inner thighs, a powerful reminder of everything she'd missed for as long as she could remember.

"Mmmmm," Jamie said, smiling, her eyes glinting mischievously.

Jess felt entirely spent as she held her weak body up on the washbasin.

Her hair was a mess. She looked totally fucked. She felt Jamie's fingers withdrawing from her pussy and she felt sad for a moment at the loss of them.

Seconds later she saw Jamie's right hand in the mirror, still slick with Jess's own arousal.

"Open your mouth and clean my fingers, baby."

Jess felt her mouth open obediently and as Jamie's fingers pushed inside she sucked her own musky earthy sex in long slow licks and sucks from each and every long strong finger.

When Jamie withdrew her fingers once again and finally this time, she also withdrew her eye contact in the mirror and casually washed her hands in the basin next to Jess, before drying them on paper towels and walking nonchalantly out of the bathroom.

Jamie Nguyen... what have you done to me?

The loud squawk of Mango, her parrot, on the nightstand tore Jess from the lingering embrace of the dream.

Disoriented, she blinked at the pre-dawn light

filtering through the blinds. A dream about Jamie Nguyen? Seriously? And an oddly... satisfying one at that.

A slow smile crept across her face. Maybe the post-interview tension had been getting to her more than she realized. Still, the intensity of the dream... was she actually attracted to the gorgeous yoga instructor? It had been years since anyone had sparked such a confusing mixture of desire and competition within her.

Shrugging off the unexplainable feelings, Jess swung her legs over the edge of the bed and stretched, muscles popping as she prepared for another day of pushing her boot camp clients to their limits.

Her phone buzzed on the nightstand, snapping her attention. A message from Ultimate Body Battle.

A grin split her face as she unlocked the screen. They wanted her! Selected. No doubt about it. She'd known it.

Despite the raised eyebrows she received for her casual interview outfit, the producers seemed to appreciate her vision. They liked her boldness, her refusal to conform, her unapologetically in-your-face training style. They called her "different," and in the world of reality TV, different was exactly what they craved.

"Called it!" she muttered to herself, a surge of confidence coursing through her veins. She knew she'd be selected, there was no doubt. But a new thought wormed its way into her mind—had Jamie Nguyen been chosen too?

A part of her, the fiercely competitive part that thrived on victory, wanted Jamie on the show. This was her chance to prove that boot camp was the superior training method, to guide her team to victory and shove it in the faces of all the doubters —including, perhaps, a certain yoga-loving rival.

And, to redeem herself after what could be considered the embarrassing bathroom incident where she had let lust get the better of her and clearly submitted to Jamie.

But then there was the other part, the one awakened by the vividness of the dream. The part that couldn't help but be intrigued by the fiery yoga instructor and the unexpected spark that ignited between them in her dream. A part that wished the dream was reality.

Whatever the reason, Jess knew one thing for sure—the upcoming season of Ultimate Body Battle was going to be unlike anything anyone had ever seen. It would be a clash of personalities, a battle of training philosophies, and maybe, just maybe, something more.

Jess Thompson and Jamie Nguyen stood side by side, facing the producers and a room full of hopeful contestants with a simmering competitive spirit.

Both tall, lean and muscular. Jamie a slightly more masculine version of Jess. Her hair was darker than Jess's and up in a sleek ponytail, her brown eyes gleaming. Her make up that the producers insisted she wore was minimal. Jess's blue eyes were sparkling and her chestnut hair was glossy in a ponytail.

It seemed Jess' silent wish of having Jamie as competition worked out and she basked in her own thrill.

Wills, the head producer, cleared his throat. "Welcome everyone, and congratulations to both Jamie and Jess for making it this far!"

Jess, ever the showstopper, flashed a dazzling smile, her toned arms gleaming under the harsh fluorescent lights.

Wills continued, "As you all know, Ultimate Body Battle is about pushing boundaries and finding the right fit."

"The format's a little different this year. We're giving you both the chance to shine. Each of you will have ten spots on your team," Sophia added.

Jess perked up, a triumphant glint in her eye. Ten chances to mold these newbies into lean, mean, boot camp fighting machines.

"Here's the deal. You'll each get a chance to pitch your training philosophies to the contestants. After that, it's up to them to choose which team they want to be on," Terry said.

David added, "Think of it as a chance to sell yourself and your approach to fitness. The contestants are looking for a coach who can help them achieve their goals, someone who inspires them."

A slow smile spread across Jess' face. Selling herself? Inspiring others? Piece of cake.

She glanced at Jamie, whose expression remained unreadable. A silent challenge passed between them. May the best trainer win. The games were about to begin.

⁓

Jess stepped forward, her athletic confidence radiating outwards. She scanned the faces before her, a predatory gleam in her eyes.

"Alright, listen up, team!" she boomed, her voice a commanding echo. "Are you tired of feeling sluggish? Fed up with fad diets and empty promises? Then buckle up, because boot camp is here to kick your butts—literally!"

A few nervous chuckles rippled through the group. Jess took it as encouragement.

"This is no walk in the park! Sweat will be shed. Muscles will scream. But guess what? You'll emerge stronger, faster, leaner versions of your-selves! Boot camp is about pushing your limits, discovering hidden reserves of resilience, and building a body that can handle anything you throw at it," she continued, her voice taking on a drill-sergeant-like tone.

She paced back and forth, her gaze locking on each participant in turn. "I'm not here to hold your hand or sing you lullabies. I'm here to push you, to challenge you, to break down your walls and build you back up, stronger than ever before. It won't be easy, but it will be worth it."

Jess finished her pitch with a triumphant smirk playing on her lips. She had laid it all out—the grit, the intensity, the promise of sculpted physiques. But as the claps died down and Jamie stepped forward, a dismissive snort escaped Jess' lips.

What did Jamie have to offer these contestants? Candles and chanting?

Jamie, dressed in a simple white tank top and black yoga pants, exuded a quiet confidence that contrasted sharply with Jess' bombastic energy.

"Thank you. Jess has presented a very... vigorous approach to fitness." A pointed look at Jess held a hint of amusement.

"My philosophy is rooted in holistic wellness. Yes, physical fitness is important, but it's just one piece of the puzzle. I believe in cultivating a connection between mind, body, and spirit. We'll work on building strength and flexibility, of course, but we'll also focus on mindfulness, stress management, and cultivating a positive relationship with your body."

Jess felt a jab of irritation. Woo-woo hippie stuff, that's all it was. She couldn't let this ethereal approach stand unchallenged. As Jamie finished, Jess practically vibrated with the need to counter.

"Hold on a second," Jess interjected, unable to contain herself any longer. "So, what happens when you're facing down a plate of greasy nachos after a tough workout? Are you going to chant your way out of temptation or actually teach these people some discipline?"

Jamie's gaze met hers, a steely glint replacing her earlier serenity. "Discipline is certainly important, but so is self-compassion. We all slip up sometimes. What matters is learning from those moments and making healthier choices in the long run. Shame and guilt are poor motivators, but self-acceptance and a positive mindset can be incredibly powerful tools for change."

The room crackled with the unspoken tension between the two trainers.

Jess felt a familiar fire ignite within her. "Positive vibes don't build muscle. They build... what? Fluffy bunnies?"

Jamie's lips thinned. "And endless negativity is a recipe for burnout. Mental well-being is just as crucial as physical strength. Can you train through chronic stress or anxiety, Jess?"

The jab hit its mark. Jess knew mental health was a valid concern, but she wasn't about to admit it in front of the contestants.

"Look, all you need is the will to win and a

good sweat session. The rest is just... Well, the rest is just fluff."

The debate had escalated quickly, leaving the contestants looking bewildered and the producers exchanging amused glances. It was clear that the battle lines were drawn, and the competition for these aspiring fitness enthusiasts had just become a whole lot more personal.

Wills boomed a hearty laugh, effectively cutting through the heated debate.

"Whoa, whoa, whoa! Easy there, tigers! This is exactly why we chose both of you. Let's be honest, Ultimate Body Battle thrives on a little bit of drama. Two contrasting training philosophies, two alpha personalities vying for dominance—it's ratings gold!"

Jess couldn't help but crack a smirk. Competition was her middle name. Jamie, however, maintained her composed demeanor.

"But most importantly, we need you to inspire these contestants, to help them find the best version of themselves, however they define it," Sophie added.

"Alright, enough chit-chat. Let's see what our contestants have to say. Line up, everyone, and choose your team!"

A ripple of excitement passed through the room as the contestants shuffled their feet, eager to make their decision. One by one, the contestants stepped forward, their decisions reflecting their own fitness aspirations.

Some gravitated towards Jess' promise of a grueling workout, eager to push their physical limits. Others were drawn to Jamie's emphasis on mindfulness and overall well-being.

In the end, a sense of satisfaction washed over both Jess and Jamie as they each found themselves with a team of ten eager participants.

"Excellent! Looks like we have a perfect balance. Now, buckle up because things are about to get real. We start filming in one week!"

A collective gasp rippled through the room. One week to prepare for the physical and mental challenges that awaited them.

"Welcome to Ultimate Body Battle, Season ten! Get ready for an experience unlike any other. This season, we're taking you out of the sterile gym and into the heart of nature—a secluded island paradise in Costa Rica!" Terry said.

"We'll be setting you up in a stunning location. Think pristine beaches, crystal-clear waters, and a backdrop of lush rainforests. This season, we're taking fitness to a whole new level—a natural level," Sophie added.

The contestants exchanged wide-eyed glances. Training under the watchful eyes of Jess and Jamie, in a secluded paradise, promised to be an experience they would never forget.

"Thanks everyone. We wish you all the best of luck. May the fittest team win!" Wills concluded.

As the contestants milled around, chattering excitedly about the upcoming adventure, Jess and Jamie found themselves face-to-face once again.

"Looks like we're in for a wild ride," Jess said.

Jamie returned the smile, a hint of steel in her gaze. "Bring it on, Jess. Bring it on."

Jess got a flashback of tasting her own slick orgasm on Jamies fingers.

Not now, Jess! For fuck's sake!

Jess puffed out her chest, a smug grin plastered on her face. "Just a heads-up, Jamie. Boot camp isn't for the faint of heart. Those yoga poses won't be enough to survive what I have planned for my team."

"Confidence is key, Jess. But sometimes, the emptiest cans rattle the loudest."

The smirk vanished from Jess' face, replaced by a scowl. "What's that supposed to mean?"

Jamie leaned in, her voice dropping to a low whisper, "Instead of attacking everyone with your rudeness and lack of manners, why don't you focus on actually preparing your team? Because come Costa Rica, you're going to get schooled."

Jess bristled. "Schooled? By you and your band of tree huggers? Don't make me laugh."

"Oh, I'm not laughing. You may have all the bravado in the world, but true strength comes from within. Look at you, huffing and puffing like a child throwing a tantrum."

Jess' face flushed crimson. "You think you can talk to me like that? I'll have you know I've built a reputation on pushing people to their limits and getting results!"

"And I've built a reputation on building well-rounded individuals, not just sweaty, overtrained machines. We'll see whose approach works better in the long run, Jess. Buckle up, because Costa Rica is about to get interesting."

"Alright, yoga fairy. Let's see how long your Zen warriors last when the real training begins."

"My team will be strong, both physically and mentally, while yours will be a bunch of burnt-out, overtrained zombies."

This woman was infuriating! "Zombies? At

least my zombies will be able to walk straight after a workout, unlike your incense-burning, chanting crew," Jess retorted.

Jamie's smile faltered for a moment, but she recovered quickly, her gaze steady. "Just because you can't handle a little introspection, Jess, doesn't mean it's not valuable. You might even learn something new down in Costa Rica, beyond grunting and lifting weights."

The competition hadn't even begun, and already sparks were flying. One week. That's all they had to prepare their teams before their unconventional showdown in the Costa Rican paradise.

One thing was certain—Ultimate Body Battle was about to witness a clash of titans, and paradise was about to get a whole lot hotter.

9

JAMIE

Stepping off the private jet, the humid Costa Rican air enveloped Jamie like a warm hug. Lush greenery stretched as far as the eye could see, the only sounds were the melodic chirping of unseen birds and the rhythmic crash of waves against the nearby shore.

"Showtime!" A sly smile tugged at Jamie's lips.

Perfect. This environment was tailor-made for her holistic approach. Here, amidst the calming beauty of nature, she could truly help her team connect with their bodies and minds.

Two sleek black vans awaited each team, whisking them away from the tourist throngs and deeper into the heart of the jungle. The paved road soon gave way to a bumpy, gravel track, the dense rainforest pressing in on either side. Howler monkeys screeched their territorial calls, a symphony of exotic sounds that filled the air.

Finally, the van lurched to a stop, and Jamie emerged, blinking in the dappled sunlight that filtered through the towering trees.

Before her lay a sight that took her breath away. A series of open-air bungalows nestled amongst the lush vegetation, their thatched roofs blending seamlessly with the surrounding jungle. Paths, made of crushed coral, snaked between them, leading to a central pavilion that sat nestled on a small bluff overlooking a crystal-clear river.

The bungalows themselves were works of rustic elegance. Polished wooden floors gleamed underfoot, and walls woven from woven bamboo panels provided a natural, open-air feel.

A gaggle of excited contestants milled about, but Jamie spotted Jess across the way, barking orders at her team to shut down their excitement. She couldn't help but roll her eyes internally. All bark and no bite, Jess.

Jamie didn't know what had come over her when she had kissed Jess in the bathroom at their interview. All she knew is that she had *really* enjoyed it. She kept having flashbacks to Jess's lovely sculpted ass all bent over and open for her and Jess's sharp blue eyes as they submitted to her in the mirror. She had looked really fucking beautiful as she came.

But fucking her into submission didn't seem to have done much for Jess's smart mouth.

Jess's jibes were constant, both in front of the camera and when they thought they weren't being filmed.

Why did Jamie find her so attractive? Jess Thompson was fucking infuriating.

A tall man with a broad smile and a mane of salt-and-pepper hair approached them. "Welcome to Casa Tranquilo, the home for Ultimate Body Battle season ten! I'm Roger, your host for the next month."

Roger, Jamie noted with approval, had a kind, calming presence. Different from the producers back in LA, all sharp edges and manipulative glee.

He led them down a winding stone path that snaked through the vibrant foliage. They emerged into a clearing, where a sprawling open-air pavilion stood amidst the trees. This was clearly where the group workouts would take place—a floor of polished wood, a thatched roof offering dappled shade, and the sound of the ocean breeze whispering through the palm fronds.

Next to the pavilion, a separate building housed a state-of-the-art gym with all the equipment one could need. A quick walk further revealed their dining area—an open-air space with communal tables crafted from local wood, overlooking a glistening freshwater pool. Already, a team of chefs scurried around, preparing a welcome feast that promised a taste of Costa Rican cuisine.

Finally, he led them to their living quarters. Two distinct structures stood nestled amongst the trees. Each lodge boasted a communal living area and individual sleeping quarters.

"Alright, superstars! This is the Boot Camp Brigade. Plenty of space for all your boot camp shenanigans," Roger announced, gesturing towards Jess' team quarters.

Jamie couldn't help but roll her eyes. Boot camp shenanigans indeed.

"And this is for Zen Warriors. A place to unwind and recharge after those intense training sessions." He points at the other structure.

Across the clearing, separated by a stone's throw, stood Jamie's and Jess' cabins opposite each other. This was a private bungalow, its exterior crafted from smooth, polished wood and adorned with hanging baskets overflowing with brightly colored orchids.

Jamie knew living in close quarters could be a recipe for disaster, especially with Jess' abrasive personality and the still concerning fact that she was so attracted to her. Jess, ever the braggart, puffed out her chest a few times, but Jamie refused to rise to the bait. She knew the real competition wouldn't be won with petty arguments but with results.

Jess unlocked her cabin, revealing a cozy space with mosquito nets draped dramatically over a king-sized bed, and a private balcony with a hammock beckoning relaxation. The bathroom, surprisingly luxurious, featured a walk-in shower with a rainfall showerhead, the promise of rinsing away sweat and stress after a long day of training.

Perfect for meditation sessions at sunrise and journaling under the twinkling stars. Jamie could already envision the positive transformations her team would undergo in this serene environment.

"Alright, teams. Get settled in! We have a welcome bonfire tonight, and the real training begins bright and early tomorrow!" Roger roared.

The first night felt less like the start of a competition and more like a tropical welcome party. A massive bonfire crackled in the center of a cleared area, casting an orange glow on the excited faces of the contestants.

Laughter mingled with the rhythmic strumming of a local band, their music blending seamlessly with the cacophony of crickets and chirping frogs.

Two long tables, laden with an impressive spread of grilled meats and fresh local vegetables, formed a barrier between the teams. Jess' "Boot Camp Brigade" sported matching red t-shirts emblazoned with a fierce-looking wolf logo, while Jamie's "Zen Warriors" donned calming blue shirts with a serene lotus flower design.

Despite the different colors and symbols, the expressions mirrored each other—a mix of nervous anticipation and thinly veiled hostility.

Jess sat at the head of her table, eyeing the offerings with a critical eye. "Alright, troops. Don't let this fancy food fool you. This is still a competition, and weakness comes in all forms. Don't overload yourselves on carbs before the real training begins," she barked, her voice echoing across the clearing.

Her team responded with a chorus of grunts and determined nods. Across the way, Jamie chuckled softly to herself.

"Remember, Zen Warriors, enjoying a healthy meal is part of taking care of your body. Savor the flavors, eat mindfully, and fuel yourselves for the challenges ahead."

The Zen Warriors mirrored Jamie's calm demeanor, their expressions relaxed and focused.

The sneers exchanged between the team members were almost comical—perfect reflections of the competitive fire burning in their coaches' eyes.

The fire roared, casting flickering shadows that danced across the faces of the gathered contestants. Jess, ever the showman, decided to seize the moment for some subtle taunts.

"Let me tell you a little story. About a time I encountered a group of, shall we say, *alternative* fitness enthusiasts." The Boot Camp Brigade roared with laughter.

"These folks were convinced that levitating was a legitimate exercise routine. Yes, you heard that right. Levitating." She paused for effect, milking the dramatic silence that followed. "So there they were, chanting and contorting themselves into pretzels, all expecting to defy gravity."

Jess' team burst in laughter, slapping their knees and hooting at their coach's tale.

Across the firepit, Jamie's Zen Warriors scoffed.

"Needless to say, they spent more time sprawled on the ground than defying gravity. But hey, at least they got a good stretch in, right?"

The Boot Camp Brigade howled with renewed laughter, their competitive spirit momentarily overshadowing the delicious barbeque that sat neglected on their plates.

Jamie, ever the master of composure, waited for the laughter to subside before playing that petty game of theirs.

"Storytime ,Warriors! Let me tell you about a group of... shall we say, *highly motivated* boot camp enthusiasts. These folks were convinced that the only way to achieve enlightenment was to climb a mountain... blindfolded."

A ripple of laughter spread across the Zen

Warriors' table, louder than their rivals' earlier laughs.

"So there they were, scaling a treacherous mountain path, completely reliant on the gruff barks of their drill sergeant to guide them."

She paused, letting the image sink in before delivering the punchline. "Needless to say, they spent more time tripping over their own feet than achieving enlightenment. But hey, at least they got a good cardio workout, right?"

The Zen Warriors burst out laughing, solidifying with each shared joke.

The contestants' bellies were full and spirits high after the taunting exchange between Jess and Jamie. The night was still young, and as if sensing the shift in energy, Roger, the host, stepped to the center.

"Time to put that delicious food to good use! Because starting tomorrow, the real competition begins. But tonight, we're all about building those teamwork muscles! I've got a series of fun little games planned that'll test your coordination, communication, and maybe even your stamina."

The contestants cheered as Roger outlined the first challenge—a relay race. Each team would be tasked with completing a series of obstacles scattered around the clearing. There would be hurdles to jump, sandbags to carry, and a hilarious coconut-walking challenge that had everyone in stitches.

"First up," Roger continued, a mischievous grin spreading across his face, "we've got a good ol' fashioned relay race! Each team will need to carry a coconut between their legs for the length of the course, tag their teammate, and hustle back. Fastest team wins bragging rights and a head start in tomorrow's training!"

A flurry of activity erupted as both teams scrambled to strategize. Jess, ever the drill sergeant, barked out orders, assigning runners based on perceived speed and agility.

"Speed is key, but don't drop those coconuts! Form matters! Don, you're first, focus on smooth handoffs! Isla, long strides, keep that nut steady! Let's show these yoga posers what real athleticism looks like!"

Jamie, meanwhile, gathered her Zen Warriors in a circle, leading them through a quick meditation session to focus their minds and bodies.

"Remember, focus on your breath, visualize your path. Let the coconut become an extension of yourselves, moving with grace and fluidity. Trust your training, trust each other, and let's have some fun!"

The first whistle pierced the air, and the clearing exploded into a frenzy.

Jess barked orders from her sideline. "Come on, move it, people! Those coconuts aren't gonna carry themselves!"

The first runner from Jess' team, a burly ex-footballer named Don, launched himself off the starting line. He held the coconut between his knees like a prized possession, but his sheer power translated to ungainly lurches.

Jess yelled encouragement, her voice a counter-point to the groans escaping Don's throat. "That's it, Don! Dig deep, feel that burn!"

Meanwhile, on Jamie's team, a slender woman named Ruby, known for her unexpected bursts of athleticism, surprised everyone. She glided effort-lessly across the course, the coconut seemingly glued to her thighs.

"Beautiful form, Ruby. Keep that focus, that breath control, you've got this!"

In the final leg, the competition tightened as

the first contestants had to compete one more run to end the relay. Don, fueled by Jess' fiery exhortations, pushed himself to a late surge. But on the Zen Warriors' side, Ruby unleashed a final burst of speed, her long stride propelling her across the finish line a hair's breadth ahead.

A collective groan rippled through the Boot Camp Brigade, disappointment written on their faces. Jess, however, saw an unexpected determination to prove themselves. She clapped her hands, her voice booming despite the loss. "Alright, Brigade! That was a good effort, but we can do better. Let's regroup and strategize before the next challenge!"

Across the clearing, Jamie offered a small smile to her victorious team. "Excellent work, Zen Warriors. Remember, even the smallest movements can lead to great victories."

The first challenge may be over, but the battle lines were firmly drawn. Both Jess and Jamie had ignited a fire in their teams—the Boot Camp Brigade's hunger to prove their strength, and the Zen Warriors' quiet confidence in their focused approach.

The night progressed with a series of light-hearted challenges—a three-legged race, a blindfolded obstacle course, and a hilarious tug-of-war that pitted teammates against each other in a battle of sheer strength.

The competitive spirit was fierce, but a sense of camaraderie began to blossom as well. Even Jess and Jamie couldn't help but crack a smile at some of the more spectacular (and often comical) failures displayed by their team members.

As the final whistle blew, Roger surveyed the exhausted but exhilarated faces around him. "See, folks? Not only did you get a workout, but you learned to work together in your teams, and that's a skill that will come in handy in the weeks to come."

The cameras were rolling throughout and Jamie had to hope to herself that they hadn't caught any of the times her gaze had drifted over Jess's body and she hoped her dirty thoughts about fucking that smirk off Jess's face were not apparent on camera.

10

JESS

The morning mist clung stubbornly to the rainforest floor as the hidden cameras strategically placed in every book and cranny panned across the clearing, giving the producers and viewers the view of what's about to go down in Costa Rica.

This was it. Day one of the real competition.

Jess stood in the training area, dressed in a sleek red sports bra, fitted black leggings and black boots. Her ponytailed hair was a chestnut mane, a perfect reflection of the competitive fire burning in her eyes. She looked incredible and she knew it.

Across from her, Jamie stood wearing flowing white yoga pants, a blue tank top and black boots. She looked amazing and Jess couldn't help her eyes straying to Jamie's firm ass in those yoga pants. Jamie's arms were also a constant source of admiration for Jess. She had beautiful muscular biceps and strong looking forearms leading to big strong hands.

All the better for bending me over and fucking me with.

Stop it, Jess!

Jamie's eyes, usually sparkling with mischief, held a steely determination. Underneath the serene exterior, a competitive spirit simmered just as fiercely as it did within Jess.

The training area was in a serene bamboo forest. Sun dappled the mossy ground, and the only sounds were the chirping of birds and the gentle rustle of leaves. Muddy trenches snaked across the ground, and a series of ropes and cargo nets promised a test of upper body strength.

Roger, the show's host, materialized in the middle of the clearing, a microphone clutched in his hand. "Welcome back, everyone! Are you ready for day one of Ultimate Body Battle: Costa Rica Edition?"

A cacophony of cheers erupted from both teams. Jess' Boot Camp Brigade roared with a raw, primal energy that sent shivers down Jess' spine.

Jamie's Zen Warriors responded with a series of enthusiastic whoops and hollers, their voices infused with a quiet confidence.

"This season, we've taken things to a whole new level. We've scoured the globe for two trainers with not just impressive physiques, but also wildly different approaches to getting you, yes YOU, into the best shape of your life!"

Cheers.

"Alright then, let me introduce your fearless leaders!"

He gestured towards Jamie, who stepped forward with a serene smile. "On the blue team, we have the embodiment of inner peace and holistic wellness—Jamie Nguyen!"

The Zen Warriors cheered, their voices a wave of gentle enthusiasm. Jess clenched her jaw, the smile on her face strained. She hated this *inner peace* nonsense.

Roger turned towards Jess, his voice booming once more. "And on the red team, the queen of hard work and determination—the one and only Jess Thompson!"

Jess stepped forward, her chest puffed out, a predator sizing up its prey. The Boot Camp Brigade erupted in a thunderous roar, their energy nearly shaking the very ground beneath them. Jess reveled in the sound, in the raw power of it all.

"Over the next eight weeks, Jess and Jamie will guide their teams through intense workouts that will test your physical limits, nutritional challenges that will revamp your relationship with food, and emotional breakthroughs that will force you to confront the mental blocks holding you back.

"Ultimately, only one team will be crowned the champions of Ultimate Body Battle: Costa Rica Edition! They'll not only walk away with the coveted title of Ultimate Body Battle Champion but also bragging rights, a hefty prize package, and maybe even some newfound self-discovery along the way!"

More cheers and applause.

"So, let's have some introductory words from each team leader!"

Jess stepped forward, her gaze sweeping across her Boot Camp Brigade. Ten eager faces stared back; their expressions determined. "This is my team! These are the warriors, the go-getters, the ones who aren't afraid to push themselves to the limit!"

The Boot Camp Brigade responded with a thunderous roar; their energy infectious.

Next, Jamie introduced her Zen Warriors. "Meet the Zen Warriors. Like a silent mountain stream, their power lies beneath the surface. They may not shout the loudest, but within them lies a focus sharper than any blade. They are warriors of the mind, ready to meet any challenge with unwavering resolve."

The Zen Warriors cheered on with yells and claps as she spoke. They formed a more subdued group, their bodies relaxed, their gazes focused.

"Great! Alright! Today, we'll be testing the two training philosophies in very different ways!"

"Jess' Boot Camp Brigade will be tackling the Gauntlet! A brutal obstacle course designed to push their physical limits and teamwork." He gestured towards a monstrous structure of walls, mud pits, and rope climbs dominating one side of the clearing.

A savage grin split Jess' face. This was her element.

"Meanwhile," Roger continued, turning towards the other side, "Jamie's Zen Warriors will be facing the Temple of Focus. A series of mental and physical challenges designed to test their inner strength and mindful movement."

There, a series of yoga mats, balance beams, and intricate rope mazes awaited Jamie's team. Her serene smile remained, but she was up for the challenge.

Turning towards her team, Jess barked out instructions, her voice leaving no room for argument. "Alright, troops! Let's go out there and show them what hard work and dedication look like! No whining, no complaining, just pure, unadulterated hustle!"

Her team responded with a chorus of grunts and determined nods. They were fired up, ready to take the Gauntlet head on.

The whistle blew, and the competition was on. Bodies scrambled over walls, splashed through mud, and grappled with ropes. Jess paced the sidelines, a drill sergeant barking out commands, urging her team forward. Every successful obstacle cleared drew a triumphant roar from her lips.

"You're a bulldozer on that wall climb, remember? Hey, don't let those monkey bars slow you down! And everyone—push yourselves! This is no walk in the park!"

She was determined to prove one thing—the

toughest competitor, the winning team, would be forged in the fires of her boot camp.

Meanwhile, Jamie's Zen Warriors moved with a different kind of energy.

"Close your eyes for a moment. See yourselves flowing effortlessly over the obstacles, strong and centered. Now, open your eyes and embody that image," Jamie said firmly.

Their movements were deliberate, focused, their faces etched with quiet determination. They may not have been the first over every obstacle, but they moved with a smooth efficiency that impressed Jess, despite herself.

"Feel your connection to the ground. Each step is a powerful statement. Move with awareness, feeling the strength in your core and the grace in your limbs."

The grueling challenge stretched on, pushing the contestants to their physical and mental limits. As the final runner crossed the finish line, collapsing in a heap of exhaustion, Jess couldn't help but let out a satisfied sigh.

The Boot Camp Brigade had finished strong, and their victory felt like a personal triumph. But as she glanced across the clearing at Jamie's team, their faces flushed but their spirits unbroken, some doubts crept into her heart. These Zen Warriors were tougher than they looked.

As the dust settled on The Gauntlet and the cheers of the Boot Camp Brigade faded, Roger reappeared on the makeshift stage.

"Alright, folks, let's give it up for both teams! You all put on a show, but there can only be one winner for today's challenge. Congratulations to the Boot Camp Brigade!"

Jess' fist pumped the air in triumph. A collective roar erupted from her team, their faces beaming with pride.

"But wait! There's more! While victory brings bragging rights, it also brings some sweet rewards." He gestured towards a group of covered tables behind him.

On the tables sat a mountain of fresh tropical fruits, alongside a cooler overflowing with refreshing coconut water.

"Enjoy the spoils of victory, Boot Camp Brigade! But remember, tomorrow brings a new challenge. And who knows, maybe the Zen Warriors will have their turn to taste victory then."

As the Boot Camp Brigade devoured the fruits and sipped on the coconut water, their victory fueling their already high spirits, Jess couldn't help but notice the sneer on Jamie's face.

Days bled into weeks, and the Costa Rican sun beat down on an intensifying competition.

Jess' Boot Camp Brigade tackled countless exercises of physical demands. They hauled heavy packs on grueling rainforest hikes, their lungs burning against the thick humidity. One day saw them sprinting across a scorching beach carrying logs, the sand sucking at their boots with every desperate stride. Another challenge involved a series of scaling walls and rope swings.

Meanwhile, Jamie's Zen Warriors faced a different kind of battlefield. One challenge involved intricate yoga sequences performed while precariously balanced on paddleboards bobbing in the crystal-clear ocean. Another challenge found them holding meditation poses for agonizingly long stretches.

Each challenge pushed the contestants to their limits, testing the effectiveness of their training styles and revealing the cracks in their individual facades. The pressure began to show, and tensions simmered beneath the surface of both teams.

Jess, moved by a relentless desire to dominate, pushed her Boot Camp Brigade to the breaking point. Her days were filled with barked orders, grueling training sessions that stretched well into the night, and a constant barrage of motivational critiques that bordered on belittlement.

"You're moving like a sloth on vacation! This isn't kindergarten playtime!"

Her team, initially energized by her drill sergeant approach, began to wilt under the relentless pressure. Faces grew strained, smiles faded, and the once enthusiastic cheers after each challenge were replaced by weary silence.

Across the way, Jamie fostered a different kind of environment. Her Zen Warriors practiced yoga routines at sunrise, their movements synchronized and graceful. They filled their bodies with healthy meals and prioritized restful sleep. Their days were filled with focused training sessions punctuated by periods of meditation and relaxation.

The contrasting approaches were evident in the contestants themselves.

The Boot Camp Brigade walked with a swagger, their muscles tensed and faces etched with determination. But beneath the bravado, a simmering discontent was brewing. Whispers of fatigue and resentment began to circulate amongst the team, especially during Jess' particularly brutal training sessions.

The turning point came during a particularly grueling challenge—a high-intensity obstacle course designed to test both physical and mental fortitude. Don, the ex-football player and Jess' star contestant, already struggling with a sore knee, tackled a challenging wall climb with a reckless abandon due to Jess' relentless shouts.

A sickening crack echoed through the field, followed by his scream. He crumpled to the ground, clutching his knee, his face contorted in pain.

The competition screeched to a halt as medics rushed to his side. The diagnosis was swift and brutal—a torn ACL, season-ending for him.

Tears welled in his eyes as the medical team helped him off the course, the dreams of victory slipping through his fingers.

The Boot Camp Brigade, their morale already teetering, sank further into despair. They all looked at her with a mixture of fear and disappointment.

Jamie, ever the pragmatist, approached Jess after the challenge. Her voice was devoid of triumph, only a quiet concern. "Maybe you're pushing them too hard, Jess? Sometimes, rest is just as important as training."

Who the fuck does Jamie Nguyen think she is?

Jess glared at her, her face a mask of fury and frustration. "They're weak. They need to be pushed! This is a competition, not a spa retreat!" Her voice, usually so full of authority, cracked with a tremor of suppressed fear.

Jess was terrified she had fucked up; she had been fighting so much harder to win, partly because of her competitive spirit and partly to push down her attraction to Jamie which was becoming increasingly challenging living in such close proximity to her.

The injury had exposed a chink in her armor. Her relentless approach, while initially impressive, had backfired spectacularly.

11

JAMIE

Jamie felt disappointed as she watched her Zen Warriors trudging back to their cabins after another lackluster performance.

They'd come in second yet again, and while there were no injuries, their movements lacked the spark, the focused intensity that had shone through during the early days of the competition.

"Maybe my approach is too... gentle," Jamie worried, sinking down onto a wooden chair on her balcony.

She'd witnessed the fire in Jess' team, the raw determination that propelled them through challenges, even if it resulted in injury. Had her emphasis on mindfulness and holistic well-being left her team underprepared, lacking the killer instinct to truly compete?

The once breathtaking view of the rainforest now seemed to mock her, a vibrant reminder of the fire that seemed to be slowly going out of her team.

Memories of their initial enthusiasm played on repeat in her mind—their quiet determination during yoga stretches, the camaraderie forged during their sunset meditations. But lately, those moments felt like a distant dream. Practices were met with sighs and half-hearted attempts. Their eyes were fixed on the approaching finish line rather than the journey itself.

Were they missing Jess' drill sergeant bark? Did they crave the external pressure, the constant push that Jess seemed to excel at delivering? A pang of doubt echoed in Jamie's chest. Had she been too focused on inner peace that she'd forgotten the competitive fire that was also a necessary ingredient?

Later that evening, Roger, the show's ever-present host, strode towards the crackling bonfire.

Jess' Boot Camp Brigade nursed their aches and pains, their faces etched with a mix of determination and fatigue. Jamie's Zen Warriors, while physically unscathed, seemed to lack the spark that had ignited them at the beginning of the competition.

"Hello, everyone. We've all been working incredibly hard these past few weeks. The competition has been fierce, the challenges demanding. But lately, something seems... off."

His gaze swept over both teams, taking in their weary faces. Jess straightened her back, her jaw clenched, while Jamie offered a small, hesitant smile.

"The producers and I have been watching. We've seen the impressive displays of strength and endurance from the Boot Camp Brigade. And the Zen Warriors, your focus and balance are truly commendable."

For a moment, the rivalry seemed to melt away, replaced by a sense of shared accomplishment.

"But something else is missing. Collaboration. Teamwork. This competition is not just about individual strength, it's about pushing yourselves and each other to new heights. And right now, that fire... well, it's flickering a bit low."

Jess' eyes narrowed, but she remained silent. Jamie shifted uncomfortably on her log.

"So, we've decided to shake things up a bit!"

A collective gasp arose from both teams. What could he possibly have in store?

"For the next week, we're merging the teams! That's right, Boot Camp Brigade and Zen Warriors will be working together as a single unit."

A stunned silence descended upon the contestants. Jess' jaw dropped, her competitive spirit momentarily stunned. Jamie's eyes widened, a mixture of apprehension and unexpected curiosity flickering within them.

"You'll be co-coached by these two formidable forces," he said to the teammates.

Roger's bombshell announcement stirred a whirlwind of emotions inside Jamie. Merging the teams? Co-coaching with Jess, the embodiment of everything she opposed? It was a recipe for disaster, a clash of philosophies that could tear the entire competition apart.

Yet, beneath the initial panic, she felt something else spark within her. Curiosity. Perhaps, there was something to be learned from this unlikely collaboration. Maybe merging their approaches wouldn't be the disaster she envisioned, but a chance to find a middle ground, a way to bridge the ever-widening gap between serenity and raw power.

Jamie stole a glance at Jess, her rival's face a mask of tightly controlled emotions. Did she see a hint of apprehension in those steely blue eyes? Or was it something else entirely?

As the fire crackled merrily, both Jamie and Jess locked eyes. A silent understanding passed between them; a grudging recognition that this unexpected twist could be a turning point in the competition.

Why do I still want to fuck her? How do I handle this?

Neither woman relished the idea of working together, but both were willing to put aside their differences for the sake of their teams. The battle between yoga and boot camp, it seemed, was about to enter a new and uncharted territory. And while the path ahead might be rocky, one thing was certain—it would be anything but boring.

The insistent clang of the camp bell echoed through the beach, its harsh tone a signal for the weary contestants to retire for the night.

Jamie, her muscles pleasantly achy after a long

day, stood for a moment, stretching her arms towards the star-studded sky.

Lost in her thoughts, she wandered towards the other side of the camp, drawn by the rhythmic crashing of waves against the shore. The moon cast a silvery sheen on the water, creating a scene of serene beauty that soothed her jangled nerves.

With a sigh, she sank down onto the warm sand, the cool night breeze a welcome caress on her forehead. The enforced disconnect from her phone, away from the constant hum of communication with family and friends, felt like a newly discovered vulnerability.

Being thrust into this competitive bubble, with only the challenges and the constant presence of her rival for company, was starting to wear on her.

A sudden crunching sound on the sand startled her. She turned, her heart jumping into her throat, only to see the unmistakable figure of Jess silhouetted against the moonlight. Every instinct in Jamie's body screamed at her to go inside or find another spot but she held her ground, forcing a mask of indifference onto her face.

Jess approached with a hesitant gait, stopping a respectable distance away. For a long moment, the only sound was the gentle lapping of the waves.

Finally, Jess cleared her throat. "Hi, Jamie."

Jamie blinked, surprised by the greeting. Had Jess actually spoken to her first? For a moment, she thought she might have imagined it.

"Hi," she finally managed. It wasn't the most enthusiastic response, but at least it wasn't a complete snub.

Jess seemed to relax a fraction. "Mind if I... sat here for a while?" She gestured vaguely towards the sand beside Jamie.

Jamie hesitated. Sitting here with Jess, under the vast expanse of the night sky, felt... surreal. But curiosity, and a hint of loneliness she wouldn't readily admit, won out. She nodded curtly.

"Nice night, isn't it? The air's cool and clean after a long day," Jess said.

Jamie, surprised by Jess' attempt at conversation, offered a hesitant nod. "Yeah, it is."

She wasn't sure what to expect from this unexpected company, but a part of her welcomed the break from the constant competitive tension.

"What brings you out here?" Jamie finally asked, her voice curious. Seeing Jess, the woman who thrived on pushing limits and barking orders, sitting quietly under the moonlight felt strangely surreal.

Jess shrugged. "Needed some air," she mumbled, kicking at the sand with her bare foot. "This whole competition thing... it's intense, isn't it?"

Jamie let out a soft laugh, a sound devoid of its usual competitive edge. "Yeah, you could say that. Especially with the... forced cohabitation starting next week."

Jess snorted. "Tell me about it. I can barely manage my own team of goofballs, let alone a bunch of Zen warriors."

A surprised smile tugged at Jamie's lips. Jess, admitting defeat? This was definitely a new side to her rival. "Well, maybe your goofballs can learn a thing or two about inner peace."

"And maybe your Zen warriors can learn the value of a good sweat," Jess retorted, a hint of her familiar competitive spirit coming back into her eyes.

They both fell silent for a moment, the playful banter giving way to a comfortable quiet. Then, Jamie spoke again, her voice softer now.

"I miss my family. My parents, my siblings... even my annoying best friend."

Jess didn't laugh this time. Instead, she nodded in understanding. "Yeah, me too. Mom, my stepdad... even my little stepbrother, the terror of the house."

They both chuckled. For a moment, they weren't competitors, they were just two women, miles away from home, facing the challenges of the competition while missing the familiar comforts of everyday life.

"Guess we're just a couple of big softies under all this tough talk, huh?" Jess said with a wry smile.

Jamie grinned. "Maybe so. Maybe that's not such a bad thing."

The waves continued their relentless crashing, the moon cast its silvery glow, and under the vast expanse of the night sky, an unlikely camaraderie began to bloom between the yoga instructor and the boot camp drill sergeant.

Jess shifted on the sand, and after a long pause, said, "You know, I wanted to apologize. For all the snide remarks, the underhanded jabs... about your approach to fitness."

Jamie blinked, surprised by the unexpected admission. "You mean all that 'gentle stretches won't win you a competition' stuff?" she asked, a hint of amusement in her voice.

Jess winced. "Yeah, that. Truth be told, I might

have been a little... territorial about my methods," she admitted with a sheepish grin.

A warmth spread through Jamie's chest. Jess, the ever-confident competitor, acknowledging a fault? It was a refreshing change.

"Well, maybe I wasn't exactly sunshine and rainbows towards your boot camp philosophy either," Jamie confessed, returning the smile.

"You know, I have to admit... I secretly admire your focus on inner peace and mindfulness. It's something I... maybe haven't explored enough," she added. Her eyes were beautiful in the evening light. Her lips were full and enticing.

Jess' eyes widened in surprise. "Really? Likewise! The dedication and raw drive you instill in your team... It's inspiring."

An unexpected silence descended between them, but this time, it was filled with a newfound understanding—a recognition of the value in each other's approach.

Jamie found her gaze dragging down over Jess's beautiful body. It was so very tempting.

"So," Jess began, "Friends?"

Jamie's smile widened, brighter this time. "Friends," she agreed, gesturing to the empty space beside her. "Come on, friend, come closer. We might as well enjoy this peace and quiet while it lasts.

Jess went closer. The tension that had hung between them for weeks was gone, replaced by a comfortable silence that felt strangely companionable.

"You know, you're... really beautiful," Jess said, her gaze fixed on the endless horizon.

"Y-you too," Jamie stammered, feeling a blush creep up her neck. "I mean, you have a kind of inner strength that's really admirable."

Both women blushed, the moonlight casting a rosy glow on their faces.

Jamie stood up. "You know what? This competition has us all hot and bothered. How about a cool down swim?" She extended a hand towards Jess.

Jess' lips curved into a smile. "You're on," she replied, grabbing Jamie's hand and letting herself be pulled to her feet.

With a whoop of laughter, Jamie stripped off and flung herself into the waves, the refreshing water washing away the sand and the lingering stress of the day. Jess followed suit, diving in with a playful splash that sent a shower of droplets towards Jamie. Jamie caught as much of a glimpse as she could of Jess's magical body. She couldn't deny that bootcamp style had done some wonders for Jess's body.

But, they were just friends, right?

For a while, they swam side-by-side, their laughter echoing across the deserted beach as they played and splashed around. Eventually their laughter calmed and the physical exertion of being in the water after a long day caught up to them. Eventually, both women emerged from the water, tired but exhilarated. They collapsed back onto the sand, their bodies slick with seawater and exhaustion.

Jamie lay on her back, staring up at the endless tapestry of stars, a smile playing on her lips. Jess lay beside her, mirroring her position. They were both breathing heavily.

"That was... amazing," Jess finally said, her voice breathless.

"Yeah," Jamie agreed, turning her head to look at Jess. In the soft moonlight, she saw a new side of her rival, a side that was playful, carefree, and undeniably attractive beyond just the physical.

Their eyes met in silence for seconds and

before either could think twice, they leaned in simultaneously, mimicking the rhythm of the waves—a slow, inexorable pull followed by a powerful crash.

Their lips met in a kiss that was both desperate and tender. It started slow, a gentle exploration that sent shivers down Jamie's spine. Jess' lips were soft, warm, and tasted faintly of salt. As the kiss deepened, a current of raw energy surged through Jamie, a potent mix of surprise and exhilaration.

They tumbled back onto the sand, a tangled mess of limbs and wet underwear- salty and sandy from the swim. The urgency escalated. Torn between the intensity of the kiss and a flicker of caution, Jamie reached for Jess' crop top, her fingers pulling underneath it and dragging it over her head. Jess responded in kind, her touch sending sparks dancing across Jamie's skin.

Jamie felt her own bra being dragged over her head. Bare skin met bare skin, as they continued to kiss with their movements mirroring the wild crashing of the waves.

Jess felt the heat between them, a wildfire waiting to ignite, and she was more than ready to fan the flames. Leaning in, she sensed Jamie's anticipation in every trembling breath. With a sly smile playing on her lips, she let her fingers do the talking, tracing slow circles on Jamie's inner thighs making her arch towards her touch.

As Jess' fingers found their mark, she reveled in Jamie's reactions, like a finely tuned instrument responding to her every touch. She knew just how to play her, teasing and tantalizing until Jamie was practically begging for more.

With a mischievous glint in her eye, she leaned in, taking Jamie's nipple into her mouth, sucking gently at first, then more urgently, unable to get enough. Her other hand caressed Jamie's breast, kneading it, feeling the hardness of her nipple against her palm.

But Jess wasn't finished yet. Oh no, she was just getting started. With a wicked grin, she moved down between Jamie's legs, dragging her underwear off. Jamie had been imagining Jess between her legs for weeks and it was finally happening. Jess dipped her head and started long slow licks of Jamie from her asshole to her clitoris, teasing with her tongue until Jamie was practically squirming beneath her touch.

"Oh fuck, Jess.... this feels so incredible."

Jamie felt Jess taking her labia in her mouth one by one and sucking them. Jamie felt Jess's hands parting her thighs further so her tongue could run lengths of her most intimate parts. Jamie felt Jess's tongue teasing and rimming and probing her anus and she thought she might explode there and then. Jamie felt Jess's tongue drag slowly back up to her clitoris and take it into her mouth and suck.

Jess felt Jamie's heartbeat racing beneath her fingertips and heard the way her breath caught in her throat as she was brought closer and closer to the edge.

And then, just when Jamie thought she couldn't take anymore, Jess pushed her fingers into Jamie's ass. Slowly, deeply, pushing inside of her as she sucked on Jamie's clitoris.

"Oh, fuck. Jess, yes...I'm so close...."

Jamie felt all the nerve endings in her sensitive ass sending bolts of electricity right through her body tangling up with the pleasure from Jess's hot wet mouth sucking at her clit. Jamie crashed over the edge into an explosive orgasm feeling herself squirt.

As Jamie cried out in pleasure and gushed all over her hand, Jess couldn't help but feel a sense of satisfaction. After all, there was nothing quite like knowing she had left someone completely and utterly satisfied.

Jamie wasn't just along for the ride; she was an active participant in this dance of desire. As she came back down to earth from the best orgasm she had had in living memory, she flipped the script, her fingers swiftly removing Jess' panties, where she was met with undeniable evidence of Jess' desire.

Jess gasped in surprise and delight as Jamie rolled on top of her, her weight pressing down deliciously on Jess and she plunged two fingers into her, igniting a firestorm of sensation that threatened to consume them both.

Feeling Jess' body responding eagerly to her touch, she reveled in the way Jess writhed and moaned on her fingers. Jamie added another finger and another and curved them upwards knowing instantly as she hit Jess's G spot and Jess immediately began to melt beneath her.

She dipped her head so her mouth was to Jess' ear.

"I've been thinking about fucking you for weeks, Jess. You are going to come so fucking hard for me, baby," Jamie whispered as her fingers fucked Jess harder and faster and Jess began to come apart beneath her.

Jamie sucked on Jess' earlobe as she continued to pin her down and fuck Jess' welcoming pussy. Her thumb was pressed tight against Jess' clitoris.

With each thrust of her fingers, Jamie pushed Jess closer and closer to the edge, until she was about to come.

And then, with a final, decisive thrust, Jess tipped over the edge, her body convulsing in a symphony of pleasure and squirting hard into Jamie's palm. Jamie watched with a sense of pride as Jess shuddered and shook, her climax washing over her like a tidal wave.

She pulled her fingers slowly from Jess and brought her hand up to Jess' mouth.

She couldn't think of anything she had enjoyed lately quite as much as watching Jess' beautiful mouth eagerly lick and suck her fingers clean.

Several moments later, they laid back cuddled in each other's arms.

"Jamie. I like you. Any chance we could take this further?"

Pulling back slightly, Jamie met Jess' gaze. "Jess, we... we shouldn't be doing this, you know that, right?"

A slow smile spread across Jess' lips, a smile that sent a thrill coursing through Jamie.

"You're right, but wouldn't it be something... a little forbidden?" She leaned in closer, her voice dropping to a conspiratorial whisper. "We could be a secret. No one has to know what happens under this moonlight."

A secret relationship, a hidden fire burning between them; the thrill of it all was intoxicating. And yet, a part of her worried about the potential consequences.

"But Jess, what about the competition? What if someone finds out?"

"We'll be careful. We'll only meet in blindspots such as here where we know there are no cameras. Besides, a little forbidden passion might just be the secret weapon we both need to win this thing." She winked.

Jamie couldn't help but smile back. The idea of facing the competition with this newfound secret simmering between them was undeniably exciting.

"Hmmm...Jess and Jamie—rivals by day, lovers by night. I kind of like the sound of that."

"So, are you saying yes to being my secret girlfriend?"

"Yes."

They laughed and leaned in for another kiss, one that spoke of the secret pact sealed under the watchful gaze of the moon.

With one last lingering look, they pulled away, they turned and walked back towards the camp, with the rhythm of their footsteps mimicking the steady beat of their hearts—a rhythm that pulsed with newfound passion and the thrill of the forbidden.

The Costa Rican sun beat down on the crew as they wrapped up filming for the day. Jamie, grateful for a moment of respite, wandered down to the rickety wooden dock jutting out into the crystal-clear water.

She sighed, letting the gentle rhythm of the lapping waves wash over her. Yesterday's encounter with Jess played on her mind, a secret thrill that couldn't let her sleep.

Suddenly, a deep, gravelly voice startled her. "Good morning, Hermosa!" a man greeted, his voice dripping with a thick Spanish accent.

Jamie looked up to see a tanned, weathered man with sun-bleached hair and brown eyes. He wore a worn straw hat and a smile that seemed permanently etched on his face.

"Hola," Jamie replied with a smile, her Spanish a little rusty but serviceable. "You're not part of the crew, are you?"

The man shook his head. "No, no. I am Miguel, a simple fisherman. This," he gestured towards the vast expanse of ocean, "is my office."

He settled onto the creaking dock beside Jamie, his gaze lingering on her a beat too long. Jamie, ever the friendly one, didn't mind the attention.

Miguel was a master storyteller, weaving tales that seemed to come straight out of a Hemingway novel.

"Ah, you wouldn't believe the size of the marlin I snagged last week. This beast, she was longer than my boat, with a body as thick as a tree trunk. Fought me for hours, that one did, pulling me all over the ocean like a ragdoll."

Jamie chuckled. "And did you catch her?"

"Catch her? Senorita, catching that beast was like trying to wrestle a hurricane! No, she snapped my line clean in two, leaving me with nothing but a memory and a sore arm."

"But," he continued, lowering his voice to a conspiratorial whisper, "I know just where she likes to hide. A secret little cove, untouched by most fishermen. One of these days, I'll be back for her, and that time, she won't stand a chance."

Jamie laughed.

The conversation shifted, Miguel regaling her with tales of his childhood spent exploring hidden coves and ancient ruins scattered across the island.

"This island holds many secrets, Senorita. Some beautiful, some a little... dangerous. But for those who know where to look, it offers a treasure trove of experiences. Perhaps, sometime, I could show you some of these hidden wonders."

"I'd love that."

As Miguel's stories flowed, Jamie stole a glance towards the crew area. There, perched on a nearby crate, was Jess. Her arms were crossed, her face an unreadable mask. Jamie knew that look.

It was the same look Jess sported whenever their Boot Camp Brigade lagged behind in a challenge. Only this time, it wasn't directed at the competition but at Jamie and Miguel.

Jamie felt a pang of guilt, quickly dismissed.

She and Miguel were just having a friendly conversation. But Jess, bless her competitive spirit, probably saw it through a different lens.

The conversation with Miguel continued, punctuated by Jamie's polite laughter and Miguel's animated gestures. She couldn't just walk away mid-conversation, especially since the man was a walking encyclopedia of local lore.

Finally, after what felt like an eternity, Miguel sighed dramatically. "Ah, it seems I have overstayed my welcome. Perhaps you would like to join me for a real Costa Rican meal sometime? My wife cooks the best ceviche on the island."

Jamie hesitated. "Thank you for the offer, Miguel, but I'm not sure my schedule allows for—"

Suddenly, an idea sparked in her head. "Actually, I think I might be able to make some time. Maybe tomorrow night?"

Miguel's face broke into a wide grin. "Wonderful! Meet me here at sunset. I won't be disappointed." With a wink and a final tip of his hat, he turned and sauntered away, his laughter echoing across the water.

She glanced towards Jess, who had already risen from her crate and was stalking towards her with a fire in her eyes that had nothing to do with the setting sun.

Jess reached her, stopping just out of earshot of any lingering crew members.

"Who was that?"

"Just a local fisherman, Miguel. He was telling me some stories about the island. Also offered to take me out for dinner sometime."

Jess narrowed her eyes, unconvinced. "Dinner, huh? Sounds friendly."

Jamie shrugged, playing up the nonchalance. "He cooks the best ceviche apparently. Thought it might be a fun way to experience the local culture."

"Well, have fun," she muttered, her voice devoid of warmth.

"Actually, there's enough ceviche for two. They say the sunsets here are amazing. Want to join?"

"Forget it. I wouldn't want to cramp your style."

"Are you jealous?" Jamie teased, enjoying the flustered look on Jess' face.

Jess scoffed. "Jealous? Please. I know you're not into men."

Jamie laughed. "But still, you felt a little jealous, didn't you?"

"Just remember, we still have our secret

meeting tonight, right?" Jess changed the conversation.

"Right. Don't be late."

"Wouldn't dream of it. Well, I'm going to go shower before dinner," she said abruptly, turning to walk away.

"Sure."

12

JESS

Jess woke up with a dopey grin plastered on her face. It had been like this for the past week, ever since that crazy night on the beach with Jamie.

In love? Ridiculous. Her gut churned with a foreign sensation every time Jamie's name even crossed her mind. Love was for sappy poets and reality shows, not her. So why did her heart practically do a happy dance whenever Jamie was around?

Seriously, what was this sorcery? Jamie, the yoga-loving, granola-munching antithesis of everything Jess believed in, was having this profound effect on her.

One minute, Jess wanted to pin Jamie to the nearest palm tree and the next, she found herself captivated by Jamie's quiet strength, her unwavering focus during challenges.

There was no denying it, the woman was a goddess. Gorgeous, with a smile that could light up a room, and a kindness that constantly surprised Jess. The complete opposite of Jess, that's for sure. Yet, whenever Jamie was near, a warmth bloomed in Jess' chest, a feeling so foreign it made her want to rip off her own skin.

Ugh. Breakfast. She needed food, and maybe a vat of coffee, to clear the cobwebs out of her head and tame these unexpected butterflies. She wasn't some lovesick schoolgirl. She was Jess, the drill sergeant, the competitor. Except, a competitor who snuck off to meet her rival under the cloak of darkness for some seriously naughty rendezvous.

A shiver danced down her spine at the memory. Those stolen moments with Jamie were unlike anything she'd ever experienced. Secret, intense, filled with a raw desire that both terrified and exhilarated her.

Jess entered the open-air bamboo dining hall with a growling stomach, as giggles and lively chatter bounced off the exposed wooden beams, creating a vibrant atmosphere.

The dining hall itself was a feast for the eyes. Towering, hand-hewn bamboo columns supported the vaulted ceiling, decorated with intricate woven palm frond designs. Lush green ferns and vibrantly colored orchids spilled from hanging baskets, adding a touch of life to the natural architecture.

Open sides offered a panoramic view of the surrounding rainforest, the verdant canopy reaching towards the hazy blue sky. Gentle breezes rustled through the leaves, carrying the distant calls of exotic birds.

In the center of the hall, a massive buffet table groaned under the weight of culinary delights.

Steaming banana bread mingled with platters of sliced mango and starfruit, while colorful bowls offered a selection of local nuts and dried fruits. A massive urn dispensed dark, aromatic Costa Rican coffee, the perfect accompaniment to a separate section of savory options—scrambled eggs with fresh cilantro, black beans and rice, and sizzling chorizo sausage.

The team members were scattered around the different tables, chattering excitedly about the day's upcoming challenge.

Her gaze immediately scanned the room, landing on Jamie by the buffet table, carefully assembling her breakfast plate.

They locked eyes for a brief moment, a silent exchange passing between them. It was a look that held a secret smile, a shared knowledge only they possessed.

She approached the buffet. With her eyes focused on the steaming platters, piling on a warrior's portion of bacon and sausage, she reached to grab some offerings.

Suddenly, a slender hand reached for the same platter of sliced tomatoes. Jess looked up to find Jamie's eyes already on her. They both froze, a beat of surprised amusement playing in their eyes.

Clearing her throat, Jess offered Jamie a curt nod, forcing her smile into something more neutral.

"Morning, sunshine. Hope you got a good night's sleep. You're gonna need all your energy today if you want to keep up with the real athletes."

Jamie's smile widened, the sarcastic challenge

in Jess' eyes a welcome sight. "Awfully kind of you to worry, Drill Sergeant, but fear not; I wouldn't miss the opportunity to witness the Boot Camp Brigade crumble under today's pressure."

"Pressure? The only pressure you'll feel today is the crushing weight of disappointment when you realize your little yoga stretches haven't been enough to instill strength in your team. Everyone knows Boot camp training has been taking a toll on their Zen energy."

A few of the team members chuckled, enjoying the usual back-and-forth between the instructors.

"Oh, I wouldn't be so sure, but at least my team members are learning to actually move their bodies instead of standing around contemplating their navels."

Jess scoffed. "A piece of advice. Building a salad fortress on your plate won't hold up against a real workout, you know." She taunted Jamie's food selection of eggs and veggies.

Jamie smirked. "Don't worry, Jess, my team doesn't need a fortress of greasy breakfast to conquer a challenge. We rely on inner strength and... digestion."

"Yeah right. Seems like yesterday your 'warriors' were the ones lagging behind in the obstacle course."

Jamie arched an eyebrow, piling some fresh fruit onto her plate with a flourish. "Funny, I seem to recall a certain drill sergeant getting winded on the climbing wall."

The other team members were watching with wide eyes, clearly entertained by the exchange. Jess met Jamie's gaze, a silent smirk playing on her lips. Maybe a little breakfast-time rivalry wasn't such a bad thing. It kept the charade going, and more importantly, kept the anticipation for the day simmering.

The two coaches went through the motions of picking their food, an unspoken choreography playing out. Reach for the mangoes—Jess, then Jamie. Spoon some yogurt—Jamie, then a mirror image from Jess.

For a few awkward seconds, the charade continued, punctuated by stifled snickers from the other team members who were starting to notice the odd mirroring.

Finally, the tension became unbearable. Jess and Jamie stopped mid-reach, their hands hovering over the same bowl of granola.

They stared at each other, the weight of the room's attention pressing down on them. Jess could practically feel the raised eyebrows and curious whispers. Her cheeks flushed a warm red, and she knew Jamie felt it too, the telltale pink dusting her high cheekbones.

With a forced cough, Jess broke eye contact. She moved on to the next dish, while Jamie found a seat at a table, stealing a glance as she ate.

The open-air kitchen buzzed with a nervous energy unlike anything the competitors had experienced before. Gone were the sprawling fields and polished gymnasiums of their usual training grounds.

Here, the air hung thick with the smoky aroma of roasting chilies and the earthy scent of fresh turmeric. Clay ovens, fueled by crackling logs, cast an orange glow across a chaotic symphony of mismatched wooden tables and battered metal bowls. This was the heart of a local village kitchen, their battleground for the day.

"Alright, troops! Welcome to the Nutritional Smackdown! Today, we're ditching the push-ups and lunges in favor of whisks and spatulas. Buckle up, because this is where the real competition heats up!"

A collective murmur ran through the team. A cooking challenge? This was interesting.

Roger chuckled. "Today, we're putting your knowledge of nutrition and resourcefulness to the test. But with a twist!" He paused dramatically, letting the suspense build. "You'll be collaborating... and competing!"

"Here's how it works. Each team will be presented with a basket overflowing with the finest local ingredients."

He gestured towards a large wicker basket overflowing with vibrant ingredients—plump mangoes, glistening mahi-mahi filets, purple yams, a block of aged cheddar cheese, and lots more. It was a curious mix, guaranteed to spark creativity.

"You have to work together, negotiate, and strategize to divide the bounty. Remember, communication is key! Once you have your chosen ingredients, you'll be on your own. Each team will create their own dish, showcasing your unique strengths and approaches to healthy eating."

He paused for dramatic effect, then added,

"Also, neutrality is paramount, Coaches. Today, you're not Team Jess or Team Jamie. No sideline coaching, no preferential treatment. You're here to guide both teams equally, offering your expertise and encouraging creativity." He shot a pointed glance at the two rival coaches, Jess and Jamie, who both nodded curtly.

Roger grinned. "Excellent! Now, for the judging. Each dish will be evaluated on three criteria: taste, creativity in using the mystery ingredients, and overall nutritional value. The team that scores the highest in all three categories will be crowned the Nutritional Smackdown champions!"

A roar of approval erupted from the teams. Strategy, collaboration, competition—the challenge was on.

Boot Camp Brigade, a motley crew of weightlifters and endurance runners, seemed lost amidst the unfamiliar ingredients. They moved over the plump plantains, a mountain of fiery red chilies, and a basket overflowing with plump, juicy shrimp.

"Don't be afraid to experiment. Remember, fresh vegetables are key. They add vibrancy, flavor, and essential vitamins," Jamie advised them.

Across the way, Zen Warriors, a group known for their flexibility and focus, hovered around the table like a flock of birds. They seemed drawn to the vibrant vegetables—bell peppers, crisp green beans, and a giant head of purple cabbage. A lighter approach, for sure.

"Hold on, maybe we can trade some of these onions for the chiles. You can still make a flavorful taste without overwhelming the dish," Jess advised.

The teammate considered the suggestion, with a nod.

With the ingredients divided, the teams dispersed to their designated cooking stations. Each station boasted a traditional clay comal (griddle) heated over open flames, a large clay pot for stews, and a collection of wooden utensils. It was a far cry from the high-tech kitchens they were used to, but it held a certain rustic charm.

Jess and Jamie moved between the teams, offering neutral guidance.

Boot Camp Brigade, lost in a fiery debate over

the merits of using coconut milk or achiote paste, turned to Jamie.

"Alright, listen up. Coconut milk will add a creamy sweetness, while achiote will give you a smoky depth. Think about what flavors you want to highlight in your dish."

Her straightforward explanation brought a spark of clarity to the team's eyes.

Meanwhile, Jess was surrounded by a group fretting over their lack of protein. "Don't panic! Remember, there are other ways to get protein. Beans can be a fantastic source, and they pair beautifully with those sweet potatoes you have."

Her suggestion was met with surprised smiles. The team, clearly used to focusing on meat as the main source of protein, hadn't considered the humble bean.

Despite the competition, an unexpected friendship began to bloom in the kitchen. Teams offered each other advice, shared cooking techniques, and even swapped a few ingredients here and there.

The competitive spirit was still present, but it was tempered by a newfound respect for each other's skills and a shared love for Costa Rican cuisine.

As the afternoon sun began its descent, a mouthwatering aroma filled the air. The teams presented their creations—a fiery fish stew from Boot Camp Brigade, and a fragrant coconut curry with lime-marinated fish from Zen Warriors.

It was time for judging. The judges, a panel of local chefs, sampled each dish with care. They assessed the taste, the presentation, and the creativity with which the ingredients were used. The team held their breath.

Finally, Roger stepped forward, his face unreadable.

"The winner of the Costa Rican Cuisine Clash is..." he paused, letting the suspense build, "... a tie!"

A chorus of gasps and surprised laughter broke out. Both teams had created delicious, authentic dishes reflecting different culinary philosophies.

Jess' team had impressed with their bold, flavorful stew, while Jamie's team had won over the judges with their light and balanced dish.

Jess, despite the competitive fire in her belly, couldn't help but grudgingly admit the other team had created a worthy dish. She stole a glance at Jamie, who offered a small smile in return.

Jess practically sprinted the last stretch of beach, the sand sinking softly beneath her bare feet.

Moonlight bathed the secluded cove in an ethereal glow, casting long shadows from the swaying palm trees. There, perched on a weathered driftwood log, was Jamie, a solitary silhouette framed by the glistening ocean.

Relief and a heat of something much hotter washed over Jess. All day, the memory of Jamie's laugh, the lingering warmth of their accidental brush during the challenge, had played in her head. Now, seeing her, she couldn't help herself.

With a whoop and a scream of childish glee, she broke into a run, her laughter echoing across the beach. Jamie whirled around, a surprised gasp escaping her lips before a wide grin stretched across her face. She ran towards her too and they collided in a warm hug.

The kiss that followed was both fierce and hungry.

Jess melted into Jamie's embrace, the scent of salt air and coconut shampoo intoxicating.

"Easy there, Sergeant Bootcamp," Jamie teased, her voice breathless.

"You have no idea how good it feels to be away from everyone and in your arms."

Jamie snorted. "Is that right, Drill Sergeant? You act all tough during the day, but under this moonlit sky, you're just a big softie, aren't you, Jess?"

Jess huffed, a playful punch landing on Jamie's arm. "Says the woman who practically tackled me when I walked in."

"Hey, you started it. But I must say, all that posturing on the training field hides a very... different kind of need." She smiled, her fingers trailing down Jess' arm.

Jess couldn't help but grin. "Maybe, but let's keep that little secret between us, shall we? My reputation for being a heartless taskmaster might take a serious hit if anyone found out I'm weak as a kitten when I'm alone with you."

Jamie laughed heartily. Pulling Jess close again, she murmured against her ear, "Don't worry, Sergeant. Your secret's safe with me. After all, who am I to judge? I, too, couldn't wait for a little... forbidden moonlight rendezvous."

"All day I just think about fucking you," Jamie whispered in Jess' ear and Jess felt shivers run through her body.

Being pinned down and fucked by Jamie was the greatest pleasure she had ever experienced. She was usually far too uptight to come for a partner, but with Jamie, her orgasm had been embarrassingly easy.

They sat together on the big log, arms around each other as they listened to the rhythm of the waves.

"Who knew a cooking competition could be so exciting?"

Jamie chuckled. "Honestly, I never thought I'd see the day you'd enjoy working with anyone, Jess, especially not a bunch of yoga enthusiasts."

"I know, right."

They both laughed.

Jess leaned closer, her voice dropping to a conspiratorial whisper. "Honestly, Jamie, this whole collaboration thing? It's not so bad."

"I kind of like it too. Working with you, I mean. Seeing a different side, the one that's not all drill sergeant and scowls."

"And you, sunshine," Jess said, poking Jamie gently in the chest, "are proving that yoga instructors aren't all about kale smoothies and downward-facing dogs."

A comfortable silence settled between them.

"You know, I kind of like this whole enemies-by-day, lovers-by-night charade."

"Me too, there's a certain thrill to it, isn't there?" Jess smiled.

"More like delicious torture. Pretending to hate you all day, only to come running here to fuck you at night."

"Oh, the agony, Though, I have to say, watching you desperately trying not to stare hungrily at my body on camera is quite entertaining."

Jamie barked out a laugh. "Oh, shut up."

"Business is business. A secret romance is a secret romance. Incredible sex is incredible sex." Jess tickled her.

"Stop already!" Jamie laughed and rolled Jess onto her back on the sand, her muscular right thigh pushing insistently between Jess' legs pressing on her clitoris deliciously.

Jess opened her legs obediently and looked dreamily into Jamie's eyes.

"Fuck me," she whispered.

Jamie took both of her wrists in her strong left hand and pinned them above her head, dipping her mouth to bite Jess' nipple through her shirt. Jess gasped in delight.

"With pleasure," Jamie whispered, her beautiful brown eyes shining hungrily in the moonlight and Jess shuddered and felt the familiar wetness of desire seeping between her legs.

13

JAMIE

Being there, with Jess, fucking her under the cloak of the Costa Rican night, was the single most delicious part of her day. Watching Jess laugh. Swimming nude in the moonlit ocean with her. Feeling Jess come and come and come again for Jamie's fingers, for her tongue was the most beautiful pleasure she could imagine. Everything else—the grueling workouts, the forced smiles, the manufactured drama—paled in comparison to these stolen moments.

But she was a bit afraid. What if someone saw them? What if a hidden camera caught a glimpse of their forbidden connection?

The producers thrived on their supposed animosity. She winced, remembering the stern

warnings about disqualification if any form of inti-
macy was discovered. The show needed their
rivalry, not a budding romance.

"Enemy fitness trainers" they'd called it, a
storyline designed to keep the viewers hooked.
And hooked they were. The ratings were through
the roof, fueled by the constant sniping and thinly
veiled hostility between Jess and Jamie.

Yet, here she was, a secret blooming in her
chest, a forbidden truth whispered under the cloak
of night. Every stolen glance across the training
field, every barb that held a hidden meaning—it
was all a game, a thrilling dance on the edge of a
knife.

They'd take the risk. They had to. Jamie
couldn't imagine a world where stolen kisses
under the moonlight were all she had.

"Just a few more weeks," Jamie whispered to
the moon.

The show would end eventually, and she
yearned for the day they could finally step out of
the shadows, their love story a melody played in
the light of day.

Until then, they would continue their secret
dance, savoring each stolen moment, a testament
to a love that defied the rules of the game.

"Alright, Sunshine. What's the plan for the night?" Jess asked.

"Actually, Miguel is supposed to pick us up any minute now. Remember he invited us for dinner with his family on the other side of the river."

Jess' smile faltered slightly. Dinner with Miguel? The ever-enthusiastic host who seemed oblivious to the simmering sexual tension between the coaches. It had completely slipped her mind.

"Oh, right. Miguel's family dinner. Sounds... fun."

"Yeah. Can't wait to meet his family, you know."

Leaning in close to Jamie's ear, she lowered her voice to a seductive whisper. "Or we could scrap the family dinner with the random island guy and instead, spend the night... tasting each other?"

Jamie yelped, swatting at Jess' arm with a playful groan. "Oh, stop it! You get more than enough sex. Miguel will be here any minute."

"Fine. Family dinner it is," Jess groaned.

A sudden shout called from across the shore. "Hola, chicas!"

Jess and Jamie spotted Miguel, standing at the

helm of a small wooden boat bobbing gently near the shore.

Moonlight glinted off the silver medallion hanging from a thick, braided leather cord around his neck.

Dressed in the traditional garb of a Costa Rican fisherman, Miguel wore a loose-fitting guayabera shirt, with the sleeves rolled up to his elbows. A wide-brimmed straw hat sat perched on his head at a jaunty angle. A worn leather band held a collection of colorful feathers tucked beneath the hatband—a souvenir from a past fishing expedition, perhaps.

"Miguel!" Jamie called back with a smile. Jess, too, couldn't help but relax at the sight of their friendly host.

They hurried towards the water's edge, and with a little help, they clambered aboard.

Settling back at the helm, he expertly steered the boat away from the shore.

"Sorry I'm a bit late. But well done, Jamie," he said, his gaze lingering on Jess. "Bringing your friend along, the stoic one. Though, I must admit, seeing you two together after all the fireworks on the show, it's a bit of a surprise!"

"Oh, right," she said quickly, "We just became

friends recently, you know, getting to know each other outside the competition." A silent plea hung in her voice—please, keep it a secret.

"Well, that's certainly a twist the producers wouldn't be expecting! But hey," he continued, lowering his voice to a conspiratorial whisper, "secrets are safe with me. Just consider this an off-camera bonus round, friendship edition!"

Jamie let out a relieved breath.

"Hola, Jess. Welcome aboard! Don't let Jamie fool you, I know you're the real brains of the operation behind all that brawn."

Jess, caught slightly off guard by his direct address, could only offer a surprised laugh. "Nice to meet you properly, Miguel. And for the record, Jamie can hold her own just fine."

A playful glance darted towards Jamie, who winked in response.

Miguel chuckled again. "Plenty of time for you both to prove yourselves later, but for now, let's enjoy this beautiful night and some good food. Isabella's outdone herself tonight. She's been in the kitchen all day, preparing a feast fit for kings! Enough food to feed a small army, she says."

"Sounds wonderful, Miguel. We can't wait to try it all," Jamie says.

Miguel nodded, then leaned in conspiratorially. "Just a heads up. Maybe don't mention the
surprise to Isabella yet. She loves planning these
big reveals."

Jess and Jamie burst into laughter, exchanging
a knowing glance.

"Our lips are sealed, Miguel. We wouldn't
dream of spoiling your wife's grand finale," Jess
assured him.

With a final chuckle, Miguel pushed off from
the shore, the gentle rocking of the boat towards
the other end.

The rhythmic lap of water against the boat lulled
them into a comfortable silence, the only sound
the gentle creak of the wood and the distant
chirping of nocturnal insects.

As they neared the opposite shore, the outline
of a small village materialized against the moonlit
landscape. Lanterns flickered warmly from a
cluster of brightly painted wooden houses nestled
amongst the palm trees.

Smoke curled lazily from thatched roofs,

carrying with it the tantalizing aromas of wood fire and spices.

The shore bustled with a quiet activity. A few small, brightly colored fishing boats bobbed gently at the water's edge, and nets, neatly mended and smelling of salt and brine, lay draped over the sides, waiting for their next encounter with the sea.

Silhouettes of villagers moved about, their laughter and the rhythmic strum of a guitar drifting across the water. A group of children, barefoot and dressed in simple cotton clothes, chased each other around.

Older men sat on weathered benches, mending fishing nets and exchanging tales in hushed voices.

As Miguel steered the boat closer, a few heads turned their way, offering friendly smiles and waves. Finally, the boat stopped by a rickety wooden pier.

"Here we are, amigas!" he announced, his voice booming across the water.

A figure emerged from the shadows at the water's edge. Even from a distance, Jamie couldn't help but smile—it was Isabella.

As the woman drew closer, she wasn't tall,

barely reaching Jamie's shoulder, and the moonlight illuminated a face sprinkled with a constellation of freckles. A cascade of reddish-brown hair
tumbled past her shoulders, a few stray strands
escaping to dance on the gentle breeze.

Her flowery dress flowed loosely around her
heavily pregnant form and her bare feet were
slightly swollen, a telltale sign of the journey her
body was making.

Holding her hand, a tiny figure toddled
towards them, giggling. The little boy, barely two
years old, was a miniature version of Miguel, with
the same dark eyes and unruly mop of hair.
Diapers, the only article of clothing adorning him,
hugged his waist.

As the boat nudged against the pier, Miguel
hopped out first, a wide smile plastered on his face.

"Mi   Amor!"   Isabella   called,   hands
outstretched.

Miguel swept her into a hug, his weathered
hand cradling her rounded belly with a tenderness
that spoke volumes of their love.

"Oh, you big goof! You nearly squashed the
baby with that greeting!"

Miguel, feigning innocence, held her at arm's
length. "The little one is strong, mi amor. Just like

its mama." He leaned in, his lips brushing her ear as he planted kisses on her.

Isabella blushed, swatting him playfully on the arm again, but the force behind it was nonexistent. "Alright, you charmer, but don't forget we have guests!"

Finally, with a chuckle, Miguel pulled away, remembering his guests. "Ah, where are my manners? Jamie, Jess, this is Isabella, my wife."

"Jamie and Jess, so lovely to have you here," Isabella said, turning her gaze towards Jess and Jamie.

Before they could respond, Isabella swept them both into warm hugs. "Welcome, welcome!"

As she released Jamie, Jamie couldn't help but blurt out, "You look radiant, Isabella!"

The compliment brought a blush to Isabella's cheeks. "Gracias, Jamie. Pregnancy agrees with some, it seems." She chuckled softly.

"Well, it definitely brings out a certain glow," Jamie continued, her gaze lingering on Isabella's face for a beat longer than necessary. Subtly, she nudged Jess with her elbow, a silent invitation to join the conversation.

Jess, not the sociable type, flashed a smile at Isabella. "Miguel mentioned you prepared quite the feast. We're both starved after a long day of... training."

"Ay, Miguel. I told you to keep that quiet! Now our guests will be expecting a royal banquet on a Wednesday night!"

Miguel chuckled, his hand reaching for hers. "Sorry, mi amor. They tricked it out of me."

Jess, caught between amusement and the slight pang of guilt for breaking the surprise, interjected with a disarming grin. "I should apologize. I guess I'm not one to keep secrets."

Isabella's exasperation melted into a warm smile. "Too bad for you then because yes, I have prepared enough delicacies to feed an army."

Suddenly, the little boy, who had been engrossed in building a sandcastle cried out as the tide threatened his creation. "Papi!"

Miguel scooped him up effortlessly, his face lighting up with paternal love.

"Hola, mi pequeño Rico," Miguel planted a kiss on the boy's forehead. "Come, let's introduce you to our guests. This is Jamie and Jess, Rico. They'll be joining us for dinner tonight."

Rico, momentarily distracted from his sandcastle project, peeked at them with wide, curious eyes. He reached out a tiny hand, and Jess, unable to resist, gently bumped fists with him. A shy smile broke out on Rico's face, and he burrowed his head back into his father's chest.

"This little rascal keeps me on my toes, that's for sure." Isabella smiles, shuffling Rico's hair.

"He's adorable."

"Just like his father," Miguel says.

Isabella beamed. "We both know he takes after me."

Miguel tried to speak but she cut him off.

"Not a word."

They all laughed.

"Come on, let's head in."

With that, Isabella and Miguel leading the way, ushered them towards a nearby house constructed entirely of bamboo. The structure glowed invitingly with warm yellow light spilling from within.

Inside, the house hummed with warmth and the comforting sounds of a family preparing for a feast.

Miguel, ever the doting husband, hovered beside Isabella, his gaze lingering on her rounded belly with an adoration that made Jess and Jamie exchange amused glances.

A soft murmur of affection passed between them, a private language of love spoken only by them.

"There you go, mi amor," Miguel placed a gentle hand on Isabella's back as she set the table. "Careful now, wouldn't want our little one tumbling out just yet!"

Isabella swatted playfully at his arm with a dishcloth. "Mi amor, you worry too much. The little one is as comfortable as a baby sloth in a hammock."

"But what if the hammock breaks, mi cielo? What then?"

Isabella burst out laughing and Miguel leaned in for a kiss. The kiss, however, turned into a full-blown smooch, complete with playful nibbles on Isabella's earlobe and a lingering embrace that made Jess and Jamie exchange amused glances.

Jess and Jamie watched the playful exchange, a warmth spreading through them as they witnessed the genuine love radiating from the couple.

"Alright, alright, you big drama king, just help me get these plantains on the table before they get cold."

Miguel grinned sheepishly. "Yes, mi amor," he replied, whisking the platter away with a flourish.

As he turned towards the table, he caught Jess and Jamie's amused smiles and winked conspiratorially.

Soon the table was adorned with a vibrant tablecloth overflowed with platters of golden patacones—thickly sliced green plantains, twice-fried to a crispy perfection, sat alongside a vibrant chimichurri sauce, colorful vegetables, glistening bowls of fresh fruit, and plates piled high with what promised to be some seriously delicious-looking grilled meats.

The first bite of the patacones sent a wave of satisfaction through Jamie. Crispy on the outside, yielding and fluffy within, they were the perfect canvas for the tangy chimichurri. Across the table, Jess mirrored her expression, a contented sigh escaping her lips.

"Isabella, this is incredible! The flavors are just... perfect."

Jess, never one for flowery language, simply nodded in agreement, a satisfied smile spreading across her face as she savored another mouthful of the savory pork.

Isabella beamed, her eyes crinkling at the

corners with delight. "Gracias, mija. Cooking is my love, and to see you both enjoying it brings me so much joy."

The conversation flowed easily as they devoured the feast, and the couple entertained them with their bickering.

Isabella's dark eyes twinkled with amusement. "Ah, yes, the competition. I hear things are getting quite heated between the two of you."

A tense silence threatened to descend, the narrative of their rivalry hanging in the balance. But before either Jess or Jamie could respond, Miguel cut in.

"Don't worry, Isabella. They're just fierce competitors. But underneath it all, I think they're secretly becoming friends."

"Forgive me for intruding but are you two a couple?" Isabella asked curiously.

A blush bloomed across Jamie's cheeks, spreading like wildfire. Jess, ever the more composed of the two, managed to ask, "How did you know?"

"There's a certain way couples move. A subtle language in the way you look at each other, the way you brush hands... it's something a woman can't help but notice."

"You're a perceptive one, Isabella," Jamie said with a weak smile.

Isabella's smile widened. "My sister, you see, she's like you both. So, I have a bit of experience recognizing love between two beautiful women."

Jamie and Jess exchanged a stunned glance. Relief at Isabella's acceptance was quickly replaced by a spark of curiosity.

"Your sister?" Jamie finally managed.

Isabella's eyes softened. "Sí," she said, nodding. "She lives in the capital city with her partner, a wonderful woman named Sofia. They've been together for many years now, and their love is as bright as the sun."

A wave of warmth washed over Jamie. Here, in a remote Costa Rican village, they'd found not only acceptance, but a kindred spirit. Jess, too, felt a weight lift from her shoulders. Isabella's words were a balm, a confirmation that their love, though hidden from the world, wasn't wrong.

"She's the one who taught me that love comes in all shapes and sizes, and it looks like you two have found something pretty special," Isabella added.

"See? Nothing ever gets past my wife. She's got eyes like a hawk, that one."

"Good thing I do, mi amor. Otherwise, who knows what kind of trouble you'd get yourself into!"

Everyone laughed, including little Rico who was playing with his food from his highchair.

In the warmth of the shared laughter, Jamie found her hand instinctively reaching for Jess' under the table.

Jess squeezed Jamie's hand back, a silent message of gratitude and unspoken affection passing between them.

14

JESS

The crisp morning air bit at Jess' exposed arms as she stood with the other contestants, facing Roger. He clapped his hands, the sound echoing through the training field.

"Alright, teams! Let's give yourselves a round of applause! You've all come a long way, and the progress has been phenomenal."

A smattering of applause followed.

Jess internally rolled her eyes. Roger's motivational speeches were starting to grate on her nerves. However, she couldn't deny she felt proud when he specifically mentioned her and Jamie's great coaching.

Roger cleared his throat, his expression turning

serious. "But, let's be honest, some of you are here for the win, not the group hugs. So, with that in mind, the collaboration experiment is officially over."

"In this final phase, we're going back to full-blown competition!"

"This next challenge is a mental marathon. A test of strategy, memory, and pure grit. This is a no-pity zone. Do whatever you can to win, as long as it stays within the rules."

Jess' competitive spirit ignited. This was her domain, the arena where she thrived. A mental challenge? Bring it on. She wasn't sure what Roger had planned, but one thing was certain—today, it was every woman for herself.

Today, she'd prove to everyone, including Jamie, that she wasn't just a drill sergeant with a sharp tongue. Today, she was a force to be reckoned with.

Roger continued, "Here's how today's challenge will work. Each team will be led by their coach, and I'll provide a starting clue that will point you towards a specific location in the rainforest."

Silence.

"Once you reach the designated spot, you'll need to search for a hidden container holding the next clue. This could involve some physical challenges, like scaling a small rock face or navigating a dense thicket."

A murmur of apprehension went through the team. Jess, however, felt excited. A little physical exertion wouldn't deter her. In fact, it might even give her an edge over some of the more... fitness-averse contestants.

"The next clue will be another riddle, leading you to the next hidden container and so on. This will continue until you reach the final location and discover the treasure chest containing a prize that will give you a significant advantage in the competition."

They gasped. The stakes were suddenly higher, the pressure amplified. This was about gaining a crucial edge in the competition.

"But wait, there's more! To add a layer of delicious chaos, we've hidden a limited number of wild card clues throughout the course."

"Finding a wild card clue, might grant you a small advantage, like skipping a particularly tricky physical challenge."

The prospect of bypassing a grueling obstacle was appealing. Jess envisioned herself confidently leading her team past a daunting rock face and the image brought a triumphant smirk to her lips.

"However, there's also a chance you might encounter a roadblock. They are physical challenges that only one team member can complete on behalf of the team. This means you'll need to strategize and decide who's best suited for that obstacle."

Finally, Roger laid out the ultimate prize. "The first team to find the treasure chest within one hour wins it all. There are actually two different paths that lead to the chest, so the first team to get there and snag it will be crowned the champions! So, are you ready to test your knowledge, your courage, and your teamwork? Let the treasure hunt begin!"

The thrill of the competition was palpable. Jess met Jamie's gaze across the room, a silent challenge passing between them. This was it. Time to outwit, outmaneuver, and outlast. The game was on.

Jess ripped open the envelope containing their first clue. The riddle, scrawled in elegant script, read:

Where the mighty river meets the salty spray, whispers of legends point the way.

Jess, with her knowledge of Costa Rica gleaned from travel shows and documentaries, immediately recognized the key elements of the riddle. The "mighty river" most likely referred to the Rio Grande, a prominent landmark in the area.

The "whispers of legends" was a trickier one. It could either be a specific beach known for its calmness or a more metaphorical reference to a secluded cove. They debated several possibilities. Could it refer to specific landmarks near the cove? Or perhaps statues or sculptures?

Finally, one of them remembered a local legend she had heard about three guardian spirits who protected a hidden path near the mouth of the Rio Grande.

Putting the pieces together, Jess concluded that the hidden path must be located near a secluded cove, guarded in some way by the location of specific landmarks or natural features.

With this hypothesis in mind, they raced towards the Rio Grande, eager to test their theory.

Their path was far from easy. A treacherous rock face, slick with morning dew, forced them to work together, their bodies forming a human chain to help each other navigate the climb. Emerging scratched and breathless, they plunged into the dense jungle, following a barely discernible trail.

Then, just as doubt began to creep in, they emerged into a clearing bathed in the golden light of the rising sun. The Rio Grande, a majestic serpent of jade green, snaked its way towards the turquoise embrace of the ocean.

Following the shoreline, they spotted a weathered signpost, half-buried in the sand. Beneath a layer of peeling paint, they discovered a small, weather-beaten box. Inside lay the next clue: *Through tangled vines and hidden doors, the secrets of the ancients roar.*

This clue sent them scrambling into the undergrowth, their path blocked by a thicket of thorny vines. With gritted teeth and determined shouts, they hacked their way through, emerging into a hidden cavern adorned with ancient petroglyphs.

Another box, cleverly camouflaged against the rock wall, held the final clue: *Where the sun meets the earth, victory awaits its rightful birth.*

Time was ticking. With a renewed sense of

urgency, they raced towards a nearby hill, their lungs burning with exertion. Reaching the summit, they were met with a breathtaking panorama—the sprawling landscape bathed in the golden glow of the mid-morning sun.

But where was the chest? Panic threatened to rise, but then Jess spotted it—a shine of metal half-buried beneath a lone kapok tree. She retrieved the final clue: a simple set of coordinates.

But there was a catch. A steep, crumbling cliff face separated them from the treasure.

A tense silence descended upon the group. This was a roadblock, a challenge that only one member could overcome. All eyes turned to Diego, their strongest climber.

His muscular frame, honed by years of mountain climbing, seemed custom-built for this obstacle—a sheer cliff face, its base shrouded in mist. The only way to access the treasure nestled on a rocky ledge halfway down was a precarious rope ladder, swaying gently in the afternoon breeze.

Diego stepped forward, his face a mask of steely determination.

Lunging forward, Jess grabbed Diego's arm before he could descend. "Diego, this is it. We've come this far, but remember, teamwork wins the game."

Her voice dropped even lower, almost conspiratorially. "Jamie told me the Zen Warrior secrets. Once you get to the cave down the cliffside, if you run into any of them, get in their way. Make them feel like there's not enough room for you both. Just trust me. We'll use their most secret fears to crush them."

Diego's eyes widened in surprise. Inside information about the other team was unexpected but welcome; he'd take any advantage he could get.

With a deep breath and a silent prayer, Diego secured his harness. The click of the carabiners echoed in the deafening silence as he edged towards the cliff's edge. The wind whipped at his face as he began his descent, a solitary figure dwarfed by the immensity of the rock face.

Minutes stretched into an eternity. Each gust of wind carried the sound of crashing waves, a chilling reminder of the danger below. Jess watched, her heart hammering against her ribs.

Doubt gnawed at the edges of her confidence. Had she made the right call? Was using Jamie's secrets a fair tactic?

Just as despair threatened to consume them, a

movement caught Jess' eye. A flicker of movement on the cliff face. Diego. He was ascending, a dark silhouette against the sun-drenched sky.

Relief washed over the team, a collective exhale of pent-up tension escaping their lips.

With a triumphant grin plastered across his face, Diego held aloft the weathered wooden chest.

They roared! They had done it! They had beaten the clock, outsmarted the competition, and conquered every obstacle in their path.

The clock ticked down the final seconds as they scrambled back down the hill, their hearts pounding in their chests. With five minutes to spare, they burst back onto the beach, the coveted chest clutched firmly in Diego's hand.

The beach, once a shared haven, now felt desolate, a reflection of the turmoil within her as the moonlight shone. Diego's successful retrieval of the chest, their team's triumphant cheers—everything seemed muted, overshadowed by the betrayal that ate at her conscience.

A rustle in the nearby dunes caught her attention. Spinning around, she saw Jamie walking towards her.

A hesitant smile stretched across Jess' face, only to falter as Jamie's expression wore a mask of fury.

She knew, with a sickening certainty, why. She'd glimpsed the devastation on Jamie's face moments after her team's loss. Now, she was here to unleash her anger. Fair and square.

As Jamie closed the distance with each forceful stride, she landed a vicious slap against Jess' cheek, leaving a burning imprint and a raw shock in its wake.

Another slap followed, quicker this time. Jess stumbled backwards, the sand cushioning her fall, the sting on her face overshadowed by the far deeper pain in her heart.

Tears welled in her eyes, blurring the image of the furious woman towering before her.

"How could you?" Jamie's voice, raw with emotion, cut through the roar of the ocean. "We were supposed to be partners. We were supposed to be..." Her voice trailed off, choked with a sob she tried desperately to suppress.

The weight of Jamie's words hit Jess like a physical blow. Shame burned hotter than the sting on her cheek. "Jamie, I..." Words seemed to fail her.

How could she explain the desperate gamble, the fear of losing, the intoxicating taste of victory that had blinded her to the cost?

"I messed up. I betrayed your trust and I'm so, so sorry," she pleaded.

"You used my trust. We shared something real, something special, and you threw it away for a stupid competition."

"Jamie, I..." she stammered, her voice barely a croak, "I didn't think it through."

Jamie scoffed, a harsh, disbelieving sound. "Liar! There's no way you just blurted all that out to Diego in a few seconds. You must've been feeding your team information all week, just in case an opportunity came, haven't you?"

"No, it wasn't like that."

Jamie let out a harsh laugh, devoid of humor. "Don't even try, Jess. I told you every doubt, every fear my team confided in me. You knew about Maya's claustrophobia, and you told it to Diego knowing she was my best choice at any moment. And you used it all against us!"

"During the cave challenge, Diego, with your intel, knew exactly what to do. He kept hovering around Maya, purposely brushing past her, talking loudly, making himself a large, imposing presence in the narrow passage. She couldn't think straight. She was trapped, suffocating. We lost precious time because of you, Jess!"

"I'm sorry—" she began, but Jamie cut her off again, her voice thick with anguish.

"Don't you dare say you're sorry!" Jamie screamed, her voice breaking. "This isn't about a simple apology. You destroyed everything! You used my trust, our connection, to win a stupid competition! My team hates me now, Jess! They think I betrayed them, that I spilled all their secrets. And you know what? I blame myself for being such a fool!"

Her voice hitched, raw with emotion. "Love must have blinded me. I regret ever falling for you, Jess. This... this secret romance has ruined everything."

The words struck Jess like a physical blow.

"Jamie, wait," Jess pleaded, her voice trembling.

"There's nothing left to say. I hate you, Jess. And I will never forgive you for this."

A raw edge crept into Jess' voice as she snapped. "Jamie, come on! This was a competition! Did you expect me to just hand you the win? If you were so worried about your team's weaknesses, you shouldn't have confided in me!" Her voice shook slightly, a tremor of guilt battling with the need to justify her actions.

Jamie recoiled as if slapped, her eyes widening in shock. "This is the real you, Jess. I was a fool to think you'd actually changed."

"You can call me whatever you want, but I've never been one to back down from a challenge. No matter what."

Jamie scoffed, a humorless sound. "So, all that love was just a way to find a weakness? A way to gain an advantage?"

Jess' heart pounded against her ribs. "No, that's not true! I..." she stammered, searching for the right words. "I really cared about you, Jamie. I still do."

But the damage was done. Jamie's face contorted with a mix of anger and hurt. "To hell with your love, Jess!" she roared. "You're nothing but a manipulator! And since your precious team won, you can shove those rewards down your throat!"

With that, Jamie turned on her heel and stormed off, her silhouette disappearing into the gathering darkness.

Tears welled up in Jess' eyes, blurring the already fading light.

She had won the competition, but at what cost?

She had clawed her way to the top, but in the process, she had lost something far more valuable —the love and trust of the person who meant the most to her.

15

JAMIE

The show's break couldn't have come at a better time. Stuck in her disaster zone of a room, she'd rather not go out nor see anyone. Clothes were strewn across the floor like fallen soldiers, empty pizza boxes stacked precariously on the floor, and an army of empty wine bottles glinted accusingly from the corner.

Jamie couldn't pinpoint the last time she'd slept or eaten anything resembling a proper meal, for that matter. Alcohol, it seemed, was the only thing keeping the deafening roar of her thoughts at bay.

It was a good thing the show had gone on a production break else how would she have faced her team? Losers. That's what they were now, thanks to her.

Worthless coach. The words echoed in her head, as she gulped from the whiskey bottle. She couldn't remember the last time she'd consumed this much, the sweet burn a dull comfort against the raging storm of emotions within.

Calls went unanswered, diverted to voicemail. Right now, all she craved was the bleak solace of solitude.

Every time her mind drifted to Jess, her fists clenched. Why did she always fall for the wrong people? Was there a flashing neon sign above her head that screamed Easy Target? The sting of tears pricked at her eyes, but she blinked them back, refusing to give in.

There was no sugarcoating it. The competition was over, the trophy likely gathering dust in Jess' gloating hands. But the real prize, her team's unwavering trust and respect, was shattered beyond repair, and it was all her fault. She'd been naive, blinded by something that felt suspiciously like... love? The thought sent a bitter laugh bubbling up from her chest. Love. What a joke.

The silence in the room was broken only by the rhythmic thud of her own heart. Lost. They'd lost, and it was all on her. The weight of that realization threatened to crush her, the guilt a bitter pill she couldn't swallow.

Jamie scrolled mindlessly through her Instagram feed, the happy faces and celebratory posts on Ultimate Body Battle was all she could see.

The entire platform buzzed with news of the finale. Jess' team, the Bootcamp Brigade, was getting all the glory.

Comments hailed Jess as a strategic genius, the *"champion of boot camp."* Articles and fan forums were rife with speculation. Some praised Jess for exploiting the Zen Warriors weaknesses, calling it a savvy game move. *"A competition is a competition,"* they argued. *"Jess won fair and square."*

Others weren't so impressed. A storm of comments trolled Jess for using underhanded tactics. *"Unethical!"* they cried. *"Not a fair battle!"* A few wild theories even popped up, suggesting a secret romance between Jess and Jamie, or that Jess was some kind of super-spy who'd infiltrated the Zen Warriors' camp to steal their secrets.

The comments took a darker turn, some criticizing the show's producers for allowing someone "*mentally unstable*" (referring to Maya's claustrophobia) to participate.

The most vicious comments slammed Jamie. "*Stupid coach*" was a phrase that kept reappearing, a painful confirmation of her self-loathing.

But there were glimmers of support too. A few messages praised her for being a "*true believer in love*," even if it backfired.

Others expressed their excitement for a "*Bootcamp Brigade victory lap*," picturing Jess hoisting the trophy aloft.

With a self-disgusted scoff, she slammed her phone face down on the bed.

The negativity was a bitter pill to swallow, but in a way, it was easier to digest than the sickening praise Jess was receiving.

Burying her head in the pillow, Jamie shut out the virtual world and its harsh judgments. Right now, all she could believe was the chorus of her own inner critic—the one that branded her a stupid coach.

And all she could think of was Jess' betrayal. She had thought there was something real building between them. She had thought she was falling in love with Jess, but none of it was real. It was all just a mirage. Clearly for Jess it had just been about sex.

She kept crying when she thought of Jess and their time together.

Jesus, Jamie. Pull yourself together.

Desperate for a break from the relentless negativity swirling in her head, Jamie stumbled out of her apartment.

Aimlessly wandering the streets, she stumbled upon a flickering neon sign that read *Open Mic Night: Spill Your Guts*. On a whim, she pushed open the door, seeking refuge in the dimly lit bar.

The bar, aptly named The Rusty Compass, reeked of stale beer and something vaguely floral, courtesy of a faded Hawaiian air freshener struggling near the dusty stage.

A mix of patrons filled the mismatched furniture—tattooed hipsters with ironic mustaches shared booths with couples on awkward first dates, all united by the flickering light of the open mic sign.

She found a seat at the back, the low murmur

of the crowd a comforting white noise. Ignoring the sticky film on the table, she ordered a drink.

On stage, a young woman with fiery red hair stood bathed in a spotlight. Then, she began to speak.

Her voice, initially shaky, gained strength as she spoke. "They say heartbreak hardens you, turns you cynical. But I refuse to believe that. This ache, this rawness... it's proof I loved, proof I dared to be vulnerable."

Jamie felt a jolt. The poet's words struck a chord deep within her. Was she allowing her bad experiences to taint her entire perception of love?

The woman continued, her voice gaining conviction. "I won't let the scars define me, make me afraid to open myself up again. Love isn't a guarantee, but it's a chance worth taking. And if someone can't handle the entirety of who I am, love flaws and all, then maybe they weren't meant to be a part of my story anyway."

Jamie listened, captivated. Each verse echoed a part of her own experience—the sting of betrayal, the self-doubt, the fear of risking love again. But the poem offered a glimmer of hope, a gentle reminder that heartbreak, though painful, didn't have to be the end of the story.

Maybe, just maybe, the poet was right. Maybe love wasn't a competition to be won, but a journey to be shared. Maybe love wasn't dead after all, and maybe, she wasn't a fool for believing in it.

As the final words faded, the young woman on stage, her eyes shining with a newfound strength, took a deep bow amidst the applause.

The applause faded, leaving a comforting silence in its wake. Jamie sat there, still lost in the echo of the poet's words, when a voice snapped her back to reality.

"May I join you?"

She turned, her breath catching in her throat. Jess stood there; a hesitant smile plastered on her face.

How? How had she found her here, in this hidden corner of the city? Had she been here the entire time?

Before Jamie could voice her bewilderment, Jess spoke again, her voice laced with a vulnerability that sent shivers down Jamie's spine. "Please, I'd like to talk to you, can you spare me a minute?"

Jamie stared at her, a whirlwind of emotions battling inside her. Finally, she found the strength to nod curtly, unable to tear her gaze away from the woman who had so deeply hurt her.

Jess slid into the seat opposite Jamie, her eyes filled with a newfound vulnerability.

"I know this is sudden, but I've been... so depressed since the show ended. I even had to see a therapist."

Jamie scoffed despite herself.

"I thought winning would make me happy, but instead, it's been a constant reminder of how I hurt you and betrayed you. I hurt the one person I cared about the most, purely to win and get good TV ratings and I have regretted that ever since."

Jamie's gaze remained fixed on the stage, a million questions churning in her mind.

"The therapist made me realize I need to find myself, to stop dwelling on the past hurt because otherwise... I might be hurting the people who care about me."

Jamie smirked. "So, the therapist finally figured out you were some ruthless mastermind."

Jess continued despite her taunt. "I, uh, actually stumbled into this bar by accident, and when I saw you walk in... it felt like... fate."

Jamie raised an eyebrow, skepticism etched on her face. "Fate?"

Jess nodded, her shoulders slumping slightly. "I know I've messed up, Jamie. I've been selfish.

The therapist called it *competitive trauma*. But that's no excuse for what I did."

A heavy silence descended upon them, broken only by the clinking of glasses from across the room. Taking a deep breath, Jess met Jamie's gaze head-on.

"Jamie, I'm sorry. I'm deeply sorry for what I did. I... I care about you. More than you can imagine. I messed up, but my feelings for you are real. I love you. I fell in love with you on that beach under the moonlight. And I just... I had to say it."

Jamie stared at her, the poet's words swirling in her mind. Forgive. Love again. Was it foolish? Was it naive? But as she looked at Jess, she decided to give it a chance.

"I'm not asking you to forgive me now, Jamie, Or maybe ever. But I had to let you know. What we shared, the way I felt... it was real."

Jamie remained silent, a battle raging within her. The hurt was still fresh, a throbbing wound. Yet, the raw honesty in Jess' eyes sparked something. Not forgiveness, not yet, but a reluctant understanding.

"I'll be heading out now," Jess finally stated, pushing herself up from the chair.

Jamie's gaze snagged on Jess' gaunt face, the

telltale dark circles under her eyes. "Why do you look like you haven't eaten in days?" she blurted out before she could stop herself.

Jess gave a helpless shrug as her only response.

Suddenly, a strange impulse took hold of Jamie. "I, uh, actually have some ground beef, ricotta cheese, and marinara sauce in my fridge. I could whip up your favorite lasagna if you want."

Jess' eyes widened in disbelief. "Really? I'd love some."

"This isn't some grand gesture. I just don't want to see a woman faint on my watch," Jamie warned, her voice hardening slightly.

"Thank you, Jamie. It means a lot."

"By any chance, did you bring your car?" Jamie asked, a hint of practicality returning to her voice.

Jess nodded. "Yeah. I'm parked a few blocks down."

"Lead the way."

As Jess walked out of the bar, Jamie followed close behind. A faint smile, barely perceptible, played on her lips. Maybe forgiveness was a long road ahead, but for now, a simple bowl of lasagna and a shared memory seemed like a good first step.

Stepping into Jamie's apartment reminded them both that the past few weeks had been difficult. Empty beer bottles and takeout containers littered the coffee table and clothes were strewn across the single armchair.

Jamie, as if sensing Jess' internal debate, offered a wry smile. "Looks like we both haven't been exactly picture-perfect lately," she said, catching Jess' eye.

"Yeah, depression does strange things to your housekeeping habits."

Jamie nodded, her expression softening. They headed to the kitchen ready to whip up a good meal when a plate slipped off Jamie's hand. It shattered with a loud snap, the sound echoing through the quiet apartment.

Jess' heart jumped, and she reacted instinctively, grabbing Jamie's hand before she could pull away. "Careful!" she exclaimed.

Their eyes locked. Without a word, Jess leaned in, bridging the gap between them.

The kiss was hesitant at first, a tentative exploration of forgiveness and a lingering spark of affection. Jamie, surprised by the suddenness, met her halfway, her touch gentle, a plea for understanding.

Jess' hand cupped Jamie's face, as the kiss deepened, a wave of emotions washed over them —regret, longing, a desperate hope for a second chance to rebuild the trust that had been so carelessly broken.

Jamie couldn't believe this was happening. The tension between them had been building throughout the car ride, but now, in the intensity of the moment, she couldn't hold back any longer.

With a surge of desire, Jess lifted her off her feet, her hands circling around her waist, and they stumbled through the living room, knocking over a lamp and a few books, but neither of them cared.

They crashed onto the couch, their lips never breaking apart. Jamie's hands were in Jess' hair, tugging and pulling her closer.

In a frenzy, they started tearing off each other's clothes, hungry to feel skin against skin. Jess' shirt was the first to go, quickly followed by Jamie's blouse, both discarded onto the floor without a second thought.

Jamie's heart raced as Jess unhooked her bra, making her breasts spill free. Jess cupped them in her hands, feeling Jamie's nipples harden against her palms.

"Damn, you're so beautiful," Jess murmured,

trailing kisses down Jamie's neck and across her collarbone.

Jamie let out a soft moan, arching her back to press closer to Jess who went on her knees between Jamie's legs, stripping her of the last of her clothes and spreading her thighs wide. Jamie felt the rush of desire along with the rush of love.

She had missed Jess, so very very much.

Jess kissed her inner thighs, teasingly close to where Jamie wanted her most. Jamie's fingers tightened in Jess' hair, urging her on.

Jess didn't need any more encouragement. She pressed her lips to Jamie's pussy, her tongue flicking out to taste her. Jamie's hips bucked in response, a gasp escaping her lips.

Jess grinned against her, loving the way Jamie responded to her touch. She sucked and licked, her hands roaming up to squeeze Jamie's breasts, feeling the hard peaks of her nipples.

Jamie was moaning louder now, her hands gripping the back of the couch for support. Jess felt her own arousal growing with every sound Jamie made and she couldn't take it anymore.

She was getting so wet that she couldn't wait to feel Jamie's tongue on her. She beckoned Jamie onto the floor where she stripped herself and adjusted her position so she straddled Jamie's face and leaned down into a 69 position.

Jamie's eyes widened at the sight of Jess' soaking wet pussy above her, and she let out a moan that sent vibrations straight to Jess' core.

"Please Jess, yes," she gasped as Jess lowered herself onto Jamie's eager mouth.

Jess felt a rush of heat as Jamie's tongue made contact, sending sensations of pleasure through her body. She shivered, but managed to focus on reciprocating, leaning down, gripping Jamie's hips and her own tongue darting out to lick Jamie's clit. She could feel Jamie's juices coating her tongue, the taste of her intoxicating.

Jess began to moan louder as Jamie sucked and licked and displayed her hunger for her. Jamie was a master at oral sex, and she knew it. Although it was harder to do with Jess's mouth working on her own pussy at the same time. She felt Jess's body responding and heard her moans and instinctively remembered how Jess liked it best. She reached her hand around and though the angle was awkward managed to penetrate Jess with her fingers while she sucked her clit.

Jess's hips rocked against Jamie's mouth, her arousal building with each passing second. Jamie's spare hand gripped her hip, guiding her movements, urging her on. The room was filled with the sounds of their mutual pleasure, their moans and gasps echoing off the walls.

Jess could feel the heat rising, and she matched Jamie's rhythm, her own fingers pressing inside Jamie and her tongue flicking over Jamie's clit with urgency.

"I'm close... so close," Jess murmured. "Come together?"

"You know what I need," Jamie growled. There was one thing that tipped her over the edge like nothing else. She trusted Jess to take her there.

Seconds later she felt Jess's finger teasing her anus and pushing inside her, exploring, probing, opening her up.

Jamie's orgasm rushed straight through her whole body, crashing over her with overwhelming force. Then Jess cried out, grinding down, her own body climaxing on Jamie's face and gushing sweetly in her mouth.

Fuck.

Jamie felt her own pleasure continuing in waves as though it might never end, and they felt linked together in new ways when Jess finally rolled off and separated their bodies,

She looked at Jamie, her face flushed and glowing with satisfaction. "You're amazing," she whispered, a smile tugging at her lips.

Jamie grinned. "I could say the same about you," she replied, pulling Jess into a deep, lingering kiss.

They pulled apart, holding each other's faces and looking into each other's eyes.

"I love you," Jess said, breathless.

"I love you," Jamie responded, her voice filled with emotion.

They hugged for a warm minute, their sweaty bodies sticking to each other.

"I'll never let you go," Jamie whispered looking into those beautiful eyes.

EPILOGUE

Jess wiped a bead of sweat from her brow as she watched Jamie lead their co-ed outdoor fitness class through a particularly grueling set of burpees.

Looking around at the mix of determined and slightly frantic faces, a wave of satisfaction washed over her.

Three years. Had it really been that long?

Finding love in the unlikeliest of places, with the fiercest competitor turned soulmate. It still felt like a story ripped straight out of a reality show, literally.

Her selfishness almost shattered everything. Yet, by some stroke of luck, she managed to claw it back from the edges.

It hadn't been easy. Rebuilding trust was like putting together a shattered vase, a painstaking process filled with apologies, awkward silences, and a lot of couple's therapy. But slowly, brick by brick, they'd rebuilt their foundation, stronger this time for the cracks.

Every morning, she woke up feeling like she'd won the lottery, not some silly fitness show trophy gathering dust on her shelf. No, the real prize stood beside her—Jamie. They'd come a long way.

The idea for the co-ed class had been a joint effort, born out of late-night brainstorming sessions fueled by take-out and shared dreams. It was a way to combine their strengths, Jamie's Zen approach to movement with Jess' high-octane, bootcamp style.

Jamie's voice, a soothing melody, drifted across the open space, guiding the group through a series of sun salutations. The contrast between Jamie's calm demeanor and Jess' energetic coaching style was stark, yet somehow, it all balanced out.

Afterwards, Jess put them through a series of killer planks and crunches, her voice hoarse with barks of encouragement.

This, Jess thought, this was magic. To see their

love translated into something that helped others, that empowered them to push their limits and discover their own inner strength. It brought a smile to her face, a smile that widened as Jamie's eyes met hers across the training ground.

Their clients often joked about getting the best of both worlds—the heart-pumping intensity of boot camp followed by the serenity of yoga. Jess couldn't help but agree. It was a perfect metaphor for their relationship.

At the end of the class, Jess felt a familiar hand brush against hers. It was Jamie, her smile as warm as the fading sunlight.

"Another successful session," Jamie said.

Jess squeezed her hand back, a silent agreement passing between them. "You know, sometimes I can't believe we almost threw all this away."

Jamie chuckled. "Me neither, babe. But hey, at least it makes the story more interesting, right?"

Jess laughed. "Definitely more interesting."

Jess led a blindfolded Jamie down a winding path. The sun had dipped below the horizon, painting the sky in hues of orange and purple. Crickets chirped a lullaby, and the air carried the sweet scent of blooming night jasmine.

"Okay, stay still," Jess whispered, stopping them at the edge of a clearing. With a flourish, she gently removed the blindfold.

Jamie gasped. Before her stood a breathtaking scene. A white gazebo, adorned with fairy lights that twinkled like a constellation fallen to earth, stood perched on the edge of a still lake, its surface reflecting the shimmering sky.

The ground beneath the gazebo was carpeted with a soft layer of rose petals in shades of pink and red, forming a perfect circle. Delicate lanterns, fueled by flickering candlelight, hung from the gazebo's roof, casting a warm glow on everything around them.

Around the perimeter of the gazebo, flower arrangements bloomed in a riot of colors: vibrant lilies, delicate orchids, and cascading bougainvilleas.

Jamie turned to Jess, her eyes wide with surprise. Jess cut a striking figure in a sleek short orange dress, her hair shining in the light and her beautiful figure evident. Jamie's desire for her was still evident and it made Jess buzz with happiness inside when Jamie looked at her with hunger in her eyes.

Jamie wore shorts and a tank top and her lean muscular legs arms and shoulders were as seductive to Jess as they ever had been.

For a moment, they stood there, speechless, the only sound the gentle lapping of waves against the shore.

Jess reached out, her hand brushing a stray curl from Jamie's cheek. "Do you like it?" she asked, her voice soft.

Jamie, her eyes shimmering with unshed tears, could only nod.

A soft smile tugged at Jess' lips as she saw the wonderment light up Jamie's face. Taking her hand, Jess guided her up the white steps of the gazebo.

As they entered, the gentle strains of a string quartet filled the air, weaving a romantic melody that made Jamie blush harder.

In the center of the gazebo, a round table draped in a crisp white tablecloth awaited them. Atop it, silver cloches covered the delicacies.

Crystal flutes sparkled with chilled champagne, condensation clinging to their sides like tiny diamonds.

Jess couldn't help but grin at Jamie's wide-eyed astonishment. Seeing her happy, truly happy, filled Jess with a warmth that chased away any lingering doubts.

"It's... it's perfect, Jess," Jamie whispered, her voice thick with emotion.

"Just like you."

The gentle melody of the strings swelled, signaling the start of a slow waltz.

Jess pulled out a chair with a flourish, ushering Jamie in. As Jamie settled down, the scent of food wafted over them, a delicious mix of herbs and spices.

Lifting the silver cloches, Jamie's eyes widened again. It was a feast fit for royalty. Salmon en papillote, its delicate aroma hinting at lemon and dill, sat next to a platter of roasted vegetables, their colors mimicking a summer sunset. A bowl of fluffy couscous, dotted with golden raisins and toasted almonds, rounded out the main course.

"Wow, Jess. Did you take a cooking class in secret? This looks incredible!"

Jess chuckled, a blush creeping up her neck. "Stop teasing. You know perfectly well I can only manage scrambled eggs and the occasional burnt batch of bacon."

They both burst into laughter.

Taking a bite of the salmon, Jamie's eyes lit up. "Seriously though, this is amazing. Every bite is an explosion of flavor."

Between mouthfuls of food, Jamie continued, "Alright, spill the beans. What do you want for your birthday this year? I promise to pull off an even grander surprise than this!"

Jess laughed, shaking her head. "It wouldn't be much of a surprise if you already knew, would it?"

"Fine. But you can at least give me a hint. Something I can work with."

Jess pondered for a moment, her gaze wandering across the star-studded sky. "Honestly, Jamie, the greatest gift you could ever give me is already here. Right here, with you, under the stars, sharing this beautiful night with the woman I love. That's all I could ever ask for."

Jamie blushed even though she tried to hide it. "Oh, come on, you can give me a hint. Anything? Spa weekend? Tickets to a yoga retreat in Bali?"

"How about we get married on my birthday? Then you wouldn't have to worry about a surprise topping this one."

Jamie's breath hitched. The playful banter evaporated, replaced by a sudden stillness.

Seizing the moment, Jess reached into her pocket and pulled out a small velvet box. With a trembling hand, she flipped it open, revealing a beautiful gold ring with small diamonds that shimmered in the light.

Taking a deep breath, Jess dropped to one knee. "Jamie, you are my strength, my partner, the love of my life. Will you marry me?"

As if on cue, the string quartet launched into a slow, romantic rendition of "Unconditionally." The melody, filled with tenderness and devotion, wrapped around them like a warm embrace.

Tears streamed down Jamie's face, a mixture of joy, relief, and overwhelming love. "Yes, Jess. A thousand times, yes!"

With a cry of joy, Jess slipped the ring onto Jamie's finger. The diamond sparkled, mirroring the tears glistening in Jamie's eyes.

"I love you, Jamie."

"I love you, Jess."

They kissed, a kiss filled with the promise of forever, a testament to a love that had weathered storms and emerged stronger.

As they pulled apart, breathless and exhilarated, the orchestra swelled into a joyous crescendo.

Jess extended her hand towards Jamie, a question brimming in her eyes. Jamie, a radiant smile illuminating her face, readily took it. Stepping into the embrace of the music, they began to sway together beneath the fairy lights, with the world around them fading away.

FREE BOOK

I really hope you enjoyed this story. I loved writing it.

I'd love for you to get my FREE book- Her Boss- by joining my mailing list. On my mailing list you can be the first to find out about free or discounted books or new releases and get short sexy stories for free! Just click on the following link or type into your web browser: https://BookHip. com/MNVVPBP

Meg has had a huge crush on her hot older boss for some time now. Could it be possible that her crush is reciprocated? https://BookHip.com/ MNVVPBP

ALSO BY EMILY HAYES

mybook.to/TCEO

If you loved this one, please do check out my CEO
Series!

Can Madison melt the heart of the icy demanding CEO
at her new job?

Printed in Great Britain
by Amazon